AQUARIUS UNDONE

ZODIAC GUARDIANS 6

TAMAR SLOAN
TRICIA BARR

JESS CONNORS PUBLISHING

Dedicated to Eric Barr by his loving wife
Tricia Barr

ERIC

The day is a gray and rainy one, the heavy sheet of water pelting the windows of Chestnut Hill. The other children are running around the common room playing tag, but Eric has never felt he belonged with them, so he doesn't join their game.

He's been at the orphanage since he was two years old, and though he has no memory of his life before, he's always felt certain that his parents—whoever they were—loved him. Maybe they died in a car crash, or some other tragic accident. Or maybe they're still out there somewhere, looking for him. Either way, he's always known he belongs somewhere else, that he didn't fit in with kids his age.

Except for Ada.

Ada, who's currently rocking in a ball in the corner, hugging her knees tightly against her.

Her bright and wild red curls look especially frizzy at the moment, and yet she still looks so pretty. The prettiest girl here. The prettiest girl he's ever seen. He knows, at eight years old, he's supposed to think girls are gross, but Ada could never be gross. Not even at this moment, when her face is sheened in sweat and paler than usual, darkening the freckles that cover her nose.

Ignoring the loud play of the other kids, Eric closes the distance between them and sits beside her, putting a comforting hand on her shoulder.

"What's wrong, Ada?" he asks.

Her eyes dart sideways at him, wide and panicked, and she scoots away from his touch.

For a moment, he falters, lowers his hand and assumes she doesn't want him near. But he can sense what she doesn't say, that she does want him there, just not touching her.

"It—it's happening again," she whimpers in a broken voice.

Eric cocks his head, uncertain of what she means. Then, as he looks closer, he can see a spark of static snapping in her curls, feel the electrical pulse she gives off like the subtle hum of a television that's been left on.

So, that's it. She's amped again. Or whatever it could be called. That's why she didn't want him to touch her. She could zap him.

He nods, trying to plaster a look of comfort on his face as he smiles at her. "It'll be okay. I'm sure it'll stop soon. Just ride it out and try to be calm."

She shakes her head and hiccups, trembling from the strain to keep herself together. "I don't understand why this happens to me. What's wrong with me? Why am I like this? Why aren't they?" She juts her chin at the kids who are glee-fully frolicking around them, ignorant to her struggle.

Eric wishes he had an answer for her. One that would soothe her and not scare her even further. But he has even less of an answer for her than he does for his own differ-ences. He doesn't know why he can do things the other kids can't, either.

Though he knows Ada isn't in pain, he closes his eyes and

focuses on her, hoping to at least alleviate her stress if nothing else.

After a few seconds, she lets out a long, shaky breath, and when he opens his eyes, he sees that she's a little less tense.

She turns her head and gawks at him. "W—was that you?"

Eric nods quietly. She knows about his secret ability, too. Their shared freakishness is why they bonded. But not why they'd grown so close. Even if she was normal, or he was normal and she was still this way, he'd be just as drawn to her, just as eager to protect her.

Her brow smooths in relief and gratitude. "Thank you."

"Any time." He attempts to put his hand on her shoulder again, and his hand is met with a tiny shock before his fingers ever reach her.

She grimaces. "Sorry."

Shrugging off the little zap, he continues the gesture anyway. He can stand a little static if it means making her feel better. "Don't worry about it."

She sighs, and he dares to scoot closer, showing her he's not afraid.

Lightning flashes in the distance, brightening the room for a split second, and a boom of thunder follows soon after. Eric looks out the window, watching the curtain of water cover it. And it makes him realize something.

"You know," he begins, "come to think of it, the last time you felt like this, it was raining. I wonder if something about the lightning amps you up."

Her brows hike up, and she inhales sharply, her eyes darting from side to side. "Oh wow, you're right! I bet there's a connection!"

Even though he can't solve the problem, he's glad he could help her figure out the cause. Or at least, the trigger. They may never know the cause. Why she emits this strange and powerful charge, or why he can alleviate pain...and cause it...

"See." He puts his arm all the way around her shoulders and gently squeezes. "As long as we stick together, every-thing will be okay."

The twinkle in her eyes dulls for a moment, doubt creeping in. Doubt that they won't be adopted together, that they'll eventually be pulled apart by circumstances beyond their control.

He's not going to let that worry her. Because nothing will keep them apart. "I'll never leave you. I promise."

The tequila goes down like it's water as Eric slams the freshly emptied shot glass onto the bar top. The first few burned like hell, but the edge has finally—mercifully—worn off.

But part of him knows that, no matter how much he drinks, or what myriad of colorful pills he swallows, this pain isn't going anywhere any time soon. Maybe not ever.

"Another," Eric says, tapping the bar.

"Joo chure, my friend?" asks the heavy-set Mexican bartender in his thick accent as he wipes the inside of a glass with a not-so-clean looking rag.

Eric nods lengthily up and down, realizing his gesture probably made him look more drunk, not less. Especially when the bartender frowns.

"How 'bout some agua, my friend?" Without waiting for Eric's retort, the man places a sweating bottle of water in front of him.

Now it's Eric's turn to frown. He doesn't want water. Water won't help him forget. Water won't take away the pain. But if it'll get him closer to that next shot, he'll take it.

He grabs the bottle, wrenches it open, and chugs it.

Despite the sweat that coats the bottle, it's not very cold. And even when he's finished it, his mouth still feels like a wad of cotton. Though that's probably from the Molly he took a few hours ago. He flicks his tongue a few times, as if the motion might make the effect go away, which it doesn't. The sticky dryness only feels more pronounced.

"I'll take another water," Eric calls. "And another shot." He gives the bartender a hostile glance.

The bartender sighs and mutters something in Spanish under his breath, then grabs another water and the Don Julio from the shelf.

Eric chugs the second water as his chubby savior reluctantly fills the shot glass with the miraculous, golden liquid, then walks away, shaking his head and muttering again. From the meager bit of Spanish Eric knows, the words are quite colorful, and they only make Eric chuckle as he picks up the shot glass and swirls the liquid around.

"You're not seriously going to drink that, are you?"

The glass slips straight through Eric's fingers and spills on the bar top.

No. She couldn't have found him. He knows all her tricks, and he's been careful to stay off the radar. Fake names, cash instead of cards, fake passport. The whole nine yards. Hell, make it twelve yards. Anything to keep her from finding him and dragging him back to a life where he has to watch her every day in the arms of a man who's not him.

All blood drained from his face, Eric turns.

Ada is perched on the edge of the bar not one foot from him, red hair wild and beautiful as ever, piercing green eyes seeing only him.

How did she get there without him seeing or hearing her? She damn sure wasn't there a second ago.

"Wh—what are you doing here?" he asks, his voice hoarse and deep.

"What do you think I'm doing here?" She flicks her thick orange curls over her shoulder and leans suggestively toward him. "We promised never to leave each other."

"I'm not the one who left," Eric accuses, mildly aware he's slurring his words.

"My friend?" The bartender looks at him, concern scrunching his round face. "Are joo okay?"

"We're fine, thank you," Eric growls. "She was just leaving."

The bartender looks even more confused, scanning the bar. "I'm sorry, who?"

Eric narrows his eyes and shakes his head. "Her." He gestures at Ada as if her presence is obvious. How could anyone miss this gorgeous redhead sitting on the bar like a phoenix perched?

"Señor, there's no one there," the bartender states slowly.

Eric blinks as he looks at him, then looks to Ada again, only to find that the bar top is completely vacant. Ada has vanished just as quickly as she appeared.

What the—

"I think joo've had enough, my friend." The bartender takes the upturned shot glass and uses the same old rag to soak up the spill.

"Oh, come on, Pablo," says a girl as she walks into the bar. "Let the man have one more drink. I promise I'll get him home safely."

Pablo eyes her for a moment, then throws his hands up. "Okay, but he's joor problem now."

The girl shrugs. "Fine by me. And put this one on my tab." She takes the empty stool to Eric's right and smiles at him. "Hi, I'm Jenn." She holds out a hand.

For a minute, Eric just stares at it, forgetting what he's supposed to do. But finally, his prefrontal cortex kicks in, and he remembers he's supposed to shake it. So he does.

"Eric," he offers in return.

"So, Eric, where are you staying?" Her voice is husky, and he's aware that she's objectively very attractive. She's tall and thin with short brown hair, body squeezed into the tightest purple tube-dress he's ever seen.

"Playa Bonita," he replies a bit robotically, still completely baffled as to what just happened.

How was Ada here one second and gone the next? Was she playing mind games with him? Even she wouldn't be that cruel after she broke his heart. Or did all their years together mean nothing now that she's found her real soulmate?

"What a coincidence," Jenn purrs. "So am I." She arches a brow and places a hand on his. "How about an after party in my room when we're done here?"

Through his drug- and alcohol-induced haze, Eric slowly realizes she's hitting on him. Though he's heard that the fastest way to get over someone is to get under someone new, he has no interest in being physical with anyone right now. He just can't.

He withdraws his hand as politely as he can. "Look, Jenn. I appreciate the drink, but I'm just not feeling like company tonight. It's nothing against you, you're very pretty. I'm just… going through something right now." Holy crap, is that the understatement of the century!

Jenn shrugs and sighs as Pablo places a fresh shot glass and a sunset colored drink in front of them. "Just my luck. The first hot American in here in a week, and he's unavailable. Story of my life." She puts the straw to her lips and takes a sip.

Eric would normally feel bad about disappointing someone, but she doesn't seem too bothered by it.

"Well…" She digs into her leather clutch and pulls out a business card. "If you change your mind, that's my cell number." Her fake purple nail is pressed onto the digits as she slides the card across the bar.

Eric accepts the card and nods, not wanting to insult her further by telling her he won't be calling. "Thanks. I'll keep that in mind."

She picks up the drink and slides off the stool. "See ya, Pablo." She waves and heads out the door. There are no open container laws in Mexico. Well, they're not really enforced if there are.

"Are you sure you don't want to take her up on her offer?"

Eric jumps and whips to his left. Ada is once again sitting on the edge of the bar. Eric's heart stops and repumps as if one of her electrical charges accidentally struck him. Or purposefully?

"She's pretty hot," Ada teases with a coy smile. "And since I'm taken, there's no reason for you not to."

Eric pushes away the full shot glass.

"Actually, Pablo, I think I *have* had enough." He stumbles off the stool and slaps a few bills on the bar. "Thanks."

"Chure thing, my friend. Buenas noches!" Pablo waves, and Eric rushes out of the dimly lit bar and onto the dark sand.

The night air is hot for this time of year, but it's still refreshing. It smells of seawater, not stale booze and sweat like inside the bar. Eric isn't sure how far Playa Bonita is from JJ's Cantina, but he figures he could do with the walk to clear his head.

"I think you should call a cab." The visage of Ada appears in front of him, floating and transparent like a ghost. "I don't think they have Uber here, do you?"

Now Eric knows he's hallucinating. He's not sure if that makes him feel better or worse. Maybe he shouldn't have taken that Molly after all. He damn sure never will again.

"Why don't you call that chick? Maybe she can give you a

ride...if you know what I mean." The Ada hallucination waggles her eyebrows playfully, and Eric slashes his hand across it, making it vanish.

"Did you think it would be that easy to get rid of me?" Her voice sounds behind him and he whips around, panic setting in. "No matter how far you travel, how many miles or years you put between us, you know I'll always be *right here*." She jabs her ghostly finger at his heart, and he swears he can feel it on his chest.

He closes his eyes, willing her to go away. "Please, just leave me *alone!*"

When he opens his eyes, he sees nothing but a dark expanse of sand and sleepy beach houses in front of him. He sighs a breath of relief. She's gone. For now.

"Turn around," her voice whispers.

He spins on his heel, certain he's going to see her figure hovering there. But instead, down the dirt road, he sees two figures in a scuffle. One is thin and lithe, and the other is large and bulky.

"No, please, stop!"

That's Jenn's voice! She's being attacked!

Eric may have snubbed her advance, but he's not going to ignore her obvious plea for help. That's not who he is.

He storms toward the figures, itching to unleash his rage on someone who deserves it.

2

ADA

"Oh honey, she looks just like you!" says the woman as she waves a cup of fruit juice and smiles at Ada.

Ada stiffens. The burly guy standing beside her could definitely pass as a red-bearded, red-haired Santa, but his hair color is where the similarities end. They'll never be like her.

He smiles widely then takes a chomp of his hotdog. "Well, hello." His gaze dips to her name badge. "Ada."

Ada molds her lips into their own smile, because she knows that's what she's supposed to do at these orphanage meet and greet barbecues. The place where the children are just as much pieces of meat on display as the food.

"Hi."

The woman moves in a little closer, her eyes bright with interest. "So, tell us a little about yourself, Ada."

Ada glances over her shoulder, the pseudo smile disappearing when she sees an elderly couple talking to Eric. The man is nodding thoughtfully. The woman's asking a question, her hand brushing over Eric's arm. Even from a distance she looks enchanted.

They like him. Of course they like him. Everyone likes Eric. He's handsome and sweet and totally unaware of how endearing he is.

And he's also sworn his heart to Ada.

"Sweetie?" the woman asks politely.

"Oh, well I'm...thirteen." Surely this couple would prefer a younger child. She wrinkles her nose. "Just reached the terrible teens."

The man blinks, but then his smile returns. "Got the red-haired temper, huh?" he says conspiratorially, pointing at his head.

"Somedays, I worry I'll explode," Ada says, straight faced.

The woman withdraws a little, her hand fluttering to her throat. She can see the seriousness in Ada's face.

If only they knew what I'm capable of...

"So, ah," the woman falters. "What are your hobbies?"

"Collecting in-flight sick bags. Which is hard, because I've never been on a plane..." Ada angles her head. "Do you two travel much?"

The couple try to hide their shocked expressions, but only partially succeed. The woman glances at the table. "Oh honey, they have that mustard you like so much!"

Ada bites her lip to hide her smile as they hurry over to the buffet table, and the woman gets another hotdog and lathers it in the generic mustard the orphanage buys by the gallon. Ada knows she should feel bad, but there's no point stringing prospective adoptive parents along. She has no desire to be taken into a fake home with fake parents so she can build a life she'll never fit into.

She doesn't have to. She has Eric.

Except when Ada turns around, she sees the older couple indicating toward Eric, a hopeful question lighting up their faces. They're asking if he'd like to go inside!

Prospective parents only do that when they think they've

found a match and they want to get to know the child better. Alone. So they can see if the connection that's budding is the foundation for a future family.

Panic pulses through Ada. She frantically looks around, then sees the power cord that goes to the speaker playing upbeat background music. The speaker that's only a few feet away from the couple trying to steal Eric.

Ada covers the few steps to the cable and picks it up. Closing her eyes for the briefest second, she sends a bolt of energy down it. They fly open when she hears the pop, then widen when she sees the arcs of electricity crackle around it.

The couple leap back in shock, the woman stumbling. The man tries to catch her as she falls backward, but she slips through his arms. She lands on her backside, her hands behind her.

Ada's frozen as the woman cries out, quickly cradling her palms to her chest.

The man helps her up, clasping her to his side as he murmurs something. Eric's gaze lands on Ada, full of 'what have you done?'

"I didn't mean for that to happen..." Ada whispers, horrified.

A worker from the orphanage hurries over, speaking to the woman as she holds her hands, her face twisted in pain. From a distance, Ada can see she's sustained some grazes.

Eric takes a step back and his eyes close.

The woman's frown instantly dissolves, and her back straightens. "I don't think the grazes are as bad as they look," she assures her husband and the worker. "They hardly hurt at all."

The worker's face is scrunched up with concern. "Let's get you inside and cleaned up."

The woman nods gratefully, and she and her husband are escorted into the square, two-story building.

Eric walks over to Ada. "I was going to politely refuse going anywhere with them," he says quietly.

Ada flushes. "I didn't think." All she saw was that she could be losing him. "I didn't mean—"

"I know you didn't," he says, his face softening. "You'd never deliberately hurt anyone."

She wishes she could hug him, but it's frowned upon here at the orphanage. Plus, she's not sure she has her powers under control after the fright. She never meant to send that much energy down the cable.

"I hate it here," she mutters.

"Yeah, me too," Eric sighs.

Ada straightens as an idea strikes her. "We should run away," she hisses, looking around to make sure no one overhears her. "Get the flock out of here."

Eric stills. "Run away? Where?"

Ada shrugs, suddenly excited about her impulsive suggestion. They could disappear, and nothing will come between them ever again. "I don't know. New York?"

It's only a train ride away, and a large city like New York is just the place for them to fall off the radar.

She grips his hand, knowing she needs to contain this excitement or more than a speaker will blow up. "Think about it. Just the two of us—no one to tell us who or what we are."

It doesn't matter that they're teens. Neither of them are normal, and they both know that.

Eric's beautiful eyes glow at the prospect. "We'll always be together."

Ada's already planning what they'll need to pack—very little considering they're orphans. "We'll find somewhere to live and a way to make some money. That's all we need."

"Just you and me," he breathes.

Ada beams. "It's all I've ever wanted."

Ada spins on her heel and paces to the other end of HQ. Flashbacks of her and Eric have been haunting her with greater and greater intensity in the days since he's been gone. Reminding her that's all she has of him right now.

History.

Memories.

A soul that cries out for its mate.

"Your agitation is growing," says a calm voice through the speakers.

Ada sighs. "You know why, Esther. I'll stop pacing when I have him back."

When she can explain to him it was all a massive misunderstanding. That she's not the Gemini Twin, and never was.

That it's him she belongs with.

Ada rubs her forehead. She royally screwed up, and now Eric's paying for it. Sure, she can control her powers. She knows who she really is—a Zodiac Guardian. But she doesn't have Eric, making any victory as hollow as her chest feels.

"The scanners are working at maximum capacity," states Esther.

Ada wonders how an artificially intelligent computer can sound so soothing. It's like she built Esther to be the comfort she unconsciously needed.

"Nothing registering around HQ or the house?"

"No changes in dark matter within the vicinity or beyond," says Esther. "I will tell you the moment there is."

Ada's lips twist. She just got put in her place by a computer.

"Okay." She glances at her watch. The sleek piece of technology is one all the Zodiacs have now—a way to communicate and track each other without being in their suits—and it tells her she's been pacing for far longer than she realized. "It's late. I'll go to sleep."

Although she knows that's a lie. Sleep has been as possible as peace of mind while Eric is missing.

"Sound plan. Good night, Ada."

Ada clasps the locket holding her peridot stone as she slowly makes her way to the doorway that will take her upstairs. She chose a bedroom at the far end of the house. She told herself it's because she needs privacy, but her secret hope is that they'll find Eric. He'll understand the mix up.

And they'll finally be together, nothing holding them back, just like they've always dreamed of.

Ada's just reached the first step when her phone flashes. She rolls her eyes. "I haven't left the room, Esther."

"My scanners are well aware of that. I thought I'd test run your most recent technological addition."

"Well, it works fine. You'll be able to contact me or any of the other Zodiacs whenever you need to."

"Excellent."

Ada places her foot on the first step, weariness battling the agitation.

"Because I have detected changes in dark matter," Esther adds.

Ada spins around and strides back into HQ. "Where?"

"Three changes, in fact. In three locations. One in New York, one in D.C., and the other in Rocky Point."

Barely breathing, Ada processes the information. In a blink, she knows where Eric is. In fact, she can't believe she didn't think of it already!

Excitement tingles through her body, for the first time in her life not manifesting along her skin.

"Tell the others, Esther," Ada says breathlessly.

She's going to get Eric back.

3

TRISTAN

Tristan enters the motel room he's staying in with Zarius and Tess, noting that their suitcases aren't unpacked. They won't be staying here in New York for long, which doesn't surprise him. They haven't found any information that suggests pods could've landed here.

What does surprise him is the way Zarius slams the old book he was reading shut.

Tess vaults to her feet. "You're back," she says warmly. "We thought you'd be doing more of a canvas of the place."

Tristan crosses his arms. "Obviously you haven't noticed how little there is to canvas." He glances at the book Zarius is trying to block with his body. "And obviously you weren't expecting me back yet."

Zarius shrugs. "It's nothing of importance, for the time being."

Tristan takes another step inside. "Then you won't mind if I have a look?"

His father quirks a brow. "You will see it when the time is right."

Tristan scowls. Zarius is using this as another one of his

lessons in patience. "I'm twelve. Whatever's in there, I'm old enough to know!"

Zarius shakes his head and Tristan feels the familiar frustration bubbling up. He knows how important it is to find the other Zodiac Guardians. Heck, one of them is his soulmate! Why won't Zarius just tell him?

Tess steps forward, her hands out in a conciliatory gesture. "Honestly, it's not that big of a deal. We're still trying to decipher the clue to the refuge."

"The refuge?"

Zarius nods, pushing to his feet. "A refuge in space. One hiding from Chardis."

Tristan's breath catches. Where others are safe from his evil?

"Except there's no record of any sightings," Zarius adds. "It could be nothing but legend."

Frowning, Tristan takes another step in, his gaze falling to the book. "Then we need to find out."

Zarius is already shaking his head. "Your focus is on learning to fight and to find the others."

"But—"

"When the time is right, then searching for the refuge will occur," Zarius states flatly, using the tone that tells Tristan the conversation is over.

Tristan huffs. "Yeah, well. I doubt we'll be finding any in New York," he snaps as he turns on his heels. "But hey, I'll go looking anyway, because that's my job."

He strides back out the door and sees a bus pulling up at the road. He breaks into a sprint, his hand up to hail it.

Tristan boards the bus and pays, stomping toward a seat then plonking himself down, arms crossed. He has no idea where the route will take him, but he doesn't really care.

He'll find out as much about the other Zodiacs as he will about the refuge.

Tristan jolts awake, the sheets twisted around his legs. He sits up in bed, cradling his head in his hands. He clings to the bittersweet images of Zarius and Tess, reveling in how real the moment felt, even if he was being a bit of a douche.

He'd forgotten they came through New York. The visit had been brief, and they'd ended up leaving in a hurry, meaning it blended with the countless other cities they moved through. And everything that had happened had seemed so innocuous...

He turns and places his feet on the floor, feeling like he needs to be grounded as if he just had one of his visions. If only he'd known back then how right Zarius was. That he just needed to be a little more patient.

And not to jump to conclusions, he thinks wryly.

New York turned out to be a goldmine of Zodiacs. There were no links to pods because Alden had buried any information to protect them. And maybe the presence of the person who had them packing should've alerted him to the interest New York was generating...

Tristan blinks in the dark, the rest of the dream sifting through his consciousness. There's a refuge out there, somewhere. And Zarius was right, they needed to focus on finding the Zodiacs all those years ago.

But the time to look for the refuge has come.

With the wormhole growing as if it's going to belch something out any second, the Zodiacs need to know if there's a safe haven for sentient beings in this Universe. It could be what makes the difference of life and death for countless souls.

Tristan shoots to his feet and pulls on a shirt. Who knows what else could be on the refuge. Maybe information on how to win against Chardis. Maybe a new way to find other Zodiacs. He glances around the room, as if the book Zarius was reading has appeared along with the realization.

First, he has to find it.

Unless it burned along with the house that had his pod in it. Tristan shakes his head. He's not going to think like that. He's going to be strategic, just like Zarius always was. He's going to have faith that it will all fall into place when it's meant to.

He steps to the door, deciding to make a list of all the places he can start searching when his watch blinks in the dark. He frowns. Ada was very clear about the colors and what each means.

Green—just letting you know, think of it as an FYI.

Orange—ah, I think we might have a situation.

Red—get your asses here now!

And the flashing light is most definitely red. He taps the screen and Esther's voice trickles out.

"All Zodiacs to HQ. Dark matter disturbance detected in several locations."

4

BRIELLE

Brielle hasn't been out of her bedroom much since Cassandra left. Cassandra had been her only friend in the orphanage, and even though their broken friendship screams at her from Cassandra's empty bed, Brielle can't bring herself to leave the space that used to feel so safe.

Especially as her twelfth birthday just passed without a word of recognition from anyone. She couldn't feel any smaller or less important.

Word has spread among the other kids about Brielle's accusation of Mr. Sinclair, and now on top of thinking she's a freak, they also think she's crazy. All she can do is curl up in her bed and weep.

No family will ever adopt her now. And she's lost the only friend she's ever had, probably forever. Cassandra didn't understand that Brielle was just trying to protect her from the visions she'd seen of Mr. Sinclair. She only hopes that he won't harm her like he did those other girls. That he'll be a true father to her, and that she'll be happy.

Even if she never speaks to Brielle again.

There's a rapping at the open door, and Brielle looks to

the hallway. Sister Agatha is standing in the doorway, her face a confusing cross between sympathetic and chastising.

"You haven't been out of this room since Cassandra left," the nun begins, the battle still raging on her face, leaving Brielle confused as to how she's supposed to react. "As your penance for dishonesty—"

"But, Sister Agatha, I wasn't—"

"As your penance for lying," Sister Agatha repeats, cutting her off. "You will tend to the garden until nightfall."

Brielle hangs her head, then nods, accepting her punishment for an innocent act of honesty that no one could possibly understand.

Maybe they shouldn't. Maybe she really is crazy.

"Come on, young lady," Sister Agatha urges, beckoning her impatiently with her hand.

Brielle sulks off her bed and follows the Sister out of her room and down the hall. As she walks after the nun like a criminal heading for the gallows, she's painfully aware of all the whispering that choruses from the other girls. She blanks them all out, trying not to hear them, but she can't help but catch the hushed "liar" here and "witch" there. They only serve to slice the wound deeper, brand her ever permanently as an outcast. A child unworthy of a true family.

When they finally make it out onto the lawn, where there are no children, only green grass, rose bushes and fresh air, Brielle almost whimpers at the relief from the snickers and jibes. Maybe she'd been a fool to stay in her room as long as she did. Maybe she should have come out here all along.

Sister Agatha grabs a pair of tree trimmers from the ground at the foot of a rose bush. "Now, what I want you to do is snip only the twigs and leaves that have grown out of shape." To demonstrate, she cuts a limb that dared to stray from the perfectly square shape of the hedge. "Chaos often tempts even the sweetest and most innocent organisms into mayhem, but with a bit of careful pruning and loving attention, even the most wayward flower may yet blossom."

Brielle isn't fool enough to doubt that Sister Agatha is making a reference to her actions. But she appreciates the pretty words all the same. Maybe it truly is chaos—or the devil, according to Sister Agatha—that makes her see these visions, that leads her toward her own destruction. Maybe if she fights it, prunes it, as the Sister says, she can make herself better.

And maybe she won't lose the next friend, if she ever gets another one.

Sister Agatha hands her the trimmers. Brielle takes them and, knowing the nun is watching patiently, scans for a branch out of place and snaps the scissors at the outline of the form. The little twig with its two young leaves falls to the ground.

"Very good," Sister Agatha praises. She pats Brielle on the back. "I'll fetch you when it's time for dinner."

She leaves, and Brielle devotes herself to her task, trimming and molding the shrubs into their desired shape with unwavering focus. Even the slightest edge of a leaf that dares to put a toe out of line, Brielle cuts it down, until one entire line is in perfect form.

When she's done with that first row, she looks down its length and admires her work. She realizes she's been so focused on this chore that she hasn't thought of Cassandra or her sorrow even once. She may even volunteer for future chores if it means freedom from those torturous thoughts.

Suddenly, there's a rustling of leaves behind her in the garden, followed by a chuckle, and she spins around.

"Hello?" she calls. To her knowledge, no one has free play outside right now. She should be the only one out here.

The whispers of her fellow orphans replay in her head, and she can't bear it out here, in the one free space she's found. "Please, just leave me alone. I'm only doing what I was told. I don't want any trouble, and if you stay out here, you'll only get us both in trouble."

A head pops up over one of the hedges. It's a boy, with brown hair and brown eyes. He looks completely average, completely normal, his boyishly cute face beaming a smile at her.

"I'm sorry," the boy says. "I don't want to get anyone in trouble. I just saw the roses from the street and thought I might get a closer look." He frowns, and he's so darned adorable that Brielle's hostility melts.

She shakes her head and puts on a smile. "It's okay." She looks over her shoulder to make sure none of the nuns are watching. Then she whispers, "If you like, you can pluck one. I won't tell." She winks, and his smile is glorious.

When he hesitates and scans the hedge, she looks for a fully bloomed rose that has blossomed out of line. She finds one, smack on top in the middle of the longest hedge. She pushes the trimmers down and cuts it at its stock, then removes the pretty pink rose and hands it to the boy.

He takes the flower and inhales its heady aroma. He couldn't be more than two or three years older than her, and clearly isn't one of them.

"What are you doing here?" she asks bluntly, realizing that any normal person wouldn't have cut right to the chase like that. She blushes at her brashness.

"I was just walking along the road," he says with a shrug, staring at the rose held close to his nose. "My dad is here on business and told me to entertain myself. I saw these flowers and just had to get closer. They really are so pretty." He glances at her, and the look he gives her makes her pulse quicken. "I like pretty things."

She all but melts on the spot. There's something different

about this boy. She can't put her finger on it, but it feels…off limits, not allowed…thrilling.

She shrugs off what she assumes is a falsely taken compliment. "Well, you shouldn't be here. If Sister Agatha sees you, she'll smite both of us with her righteous wrath."

The boy frowns in disappointment. Then something in his face changes, becomes more playful. Mischievous. "Do you ever get to play, with other kids, I mean? Are you ever allowed to leave this place?"

"Well, yes, I get to leave for school," she replies, thinking. "But I'm expected to come right back afterward."

He considers this, rubbing his chin. "Well, maybe you miss your bus some day, and you and I can hang out." He smiles cheekily. "I like you. You're different. I'd like to talk to you more."

There's no mistaking that this statement is a compliment this time, and her face burns with this one shining show of acceptance.

She swallows, trying to stifle the red that undoubtedly blazes in her cheeks. "I don't know. I've never missed the bus before." Curse her inability to lie!

The boy laughs. "Never say never, orphan girl."

"Hey," she snaps. "I have a name."

"What is it?" he asks with a wry smile.

"Brielle," she states matter-of-factly.

He reaches a hand across the hedge. "I'm Carlton."

She accepts his outstretched hand, only to find that it's a closed fist. He takes her hand and releases the contents of his fist into her hers, closing it after he does.

"See ya, Brielle." He walks away, waving.

She withdraws her closed hand with the mysterious item safely tucked within. "See ya, Carlton."

Once he's gone, she opens her hand. Inside is a woven mesh bracelet of all different colors.

Her brows hike up into her scalp.

This is the first gift she's ever been given. By anyone. And even if she never sees him again, she'll cherish it forever.

Brielle stands on the grass, fingering the worn woolen bracelet on her wrist, searching for any distraction from her grief, and from the knowledge she's up next.

"Thank you," says Sister Chastity to the crowd gathered at the cemetery. She dabs her eyes with a handkerchief, and a chorus of sniffles solutes her. She clears her throat. "And now, one of our recent adoptees, who worked closely with Sister Agatha as a volunteer during her time here, would like to say a few words."

Brielle's throat hardens to stone as Sister Chastity turns her sorrowful eyes on her.

Her feet feel like they've grown roots, locking her to this spot.

Kerrim's hand on her shoulder gives an encouraging squeeze as his voice whispers, "You've got this."

She inhales and exhales slowly, nodding. She can do this. And she really needs to do this.

Impossibly, she uproots her feet from the ground and steps toward the podium that stands beside the beautiful black casket. She takes her place behind it and looks at the tear-streaked faces, remembering that there's no room for embarrassment right now.

"Sister Agatha—" Her voice cracks, and she struggles to swallow several times before her muscles finally let her. "Sister Agatha was more than just the headmistress of the Grace Orphanage, and more than the Mother Superior of its church."

Every head in the audience bobs up and down, like

wayward hunks of wood floating on the surface of the sea after an angry storm tore their ship asunder.

"To many of us, she was the only mother any of us ever knew," she continues, gripping the podium for support. "She did everything a mother is meant to do. She provided shelter and security from a world that would hurt us. She offered comfort and support when we struggled. And sure, she punished us when we strayed at times."

She hiccups on a laugh, and several of the other orphans chuckle solemnly with her.

"But most importantly..." She bites her lip to force back the sob that's begging to break free, and holds her lips in her teeth until the urge fades. "I've never known anyone who has the immense capacity to love that she did. She loved every single person whose life she touched like they were her own children. Not even just the orphans and nuns in her charge, but *everyone*."

Brielle looks off into the pale blue sky, trying to disappear into the memory she's about to share.

"I'll never forget the first time she took me to the market with her to gather supplies after I started volunteering in the kitchen. I remember thinking it was odd that she took us to the route that would go around the back of the store, that it would've been a shorter walk if we'd just gone toward the front parking lot. But, if there's one thing everyone who knew Sister Agatha knew, it was not to question her."

A laugh bubbles out of her, and the audience laughs in sync with her, the nuns especially nodding.

"There was a homeless man sitting in the alley next to a structure made of cardboard boxes which he obviously lived in." Brielle can still see him in her mind. Long brown hair and unkempt beard matted and filthy. His once white t-shirt stained brown in various shades all over. Holes in the knees of his jeans and a toe poking out of the tip of one tattered sneaker. "Everything about the man beckoned me to look away, to assume he was somehow dangerous and to keep my distance. But, as we got closer, Sister Agatha approached him.

"Good morning, Oscar,' she'd greeted him, and held out a hand to help him stand so they could embrace. I was shocked, a little horrified, but overall mesmerized. That she not only was willing to hug this derelict man, but that she knew him by name. They bantered back and forth for a moment, and then she led me into the store like the strangest thing I'd ever witnessed hadn't just happened. We bought our groceries for the orphanage, and then headed back the same way we came.

"She stopped once again at Oscar and handed him a loaf of bread and several cans of tuna and said, 'This should hold you over for the week.' Overcome with joy, the man embraced her and kissed her cheek. Then we continued on our merry way and never spoke of it. But it touched me in a way I can never explain.

"Sister Agatha did everything she could for everyone she knew. The love in her heart knew no bounds. And I, for one, am so grateful that she shared some of it with me. She showed me *how* to love, and taught me that no one is undeserving of it." She rushes her hand to cover her mouth as a sob gushes out. "Thank you."

She runs back to Kerrim's side as quickly as she can before her knees give out. He welcomes her with an arm open and ready to wrap around her shoulders.

"That was beautiful, Brielle," Cassandra whispers behind her.

"Good job," Jareth whispers.

Brielle's soul lightens, not only because she got to say her final goodbye to Sister Agatha, but also at the knowledge that she has the support of all her friends.

"You did great, Brielle," Tristan chimes in, giving her arm a nudge, careful to make it far from where Kerrim is touching her.

She looks over her shoulder at him and returns his smile as wide as her sad lips will stretch—which isn't much. She's happy that he came. With all the weirdness that's happened between them lately, and how hard it is for them to be in each other's presence, she would've only been more hurt if he wasn't here. It's a sign that, no matter what, they're still friends, and always will be.

And it also helps that her hot new guy currently has his arm wrapped around her. Though they haven't put any labels on their relationship, and she's happy about that. She doesn't want a boyfriend right now. Kissing him makes everything else fade away into blackness, and at least for the moment, it doesn't come with the added complications of any promises that are likely to be broken. Her heart gets to stay right in the tenuous state Tristan left it, safe from further harm.

"Thank you, everyone, for your kind words about Sister Agatha," announces Sister Kathrine as she takes the podium. "The Grace Orphanage Youth Choir has offered to sing her favorite hymn while we lower her into her final resting place." She waves her hand toward the small flock of girls dressed in their choir robes, and they begin to sing "Ave Maria."

Sniffles and open sobs choke out of the crowd as the pall-bearers lower the casket into the grave. And Brielle stares at the empty shell of the woman who raised her slowly disappearing into the earth, second by painful, lingering second.

When mercifully yet cruelly, her body is fully lowered, the crowd dissipates so the gravediggers can get to work. Many are going back to the orphanage for a celebration of life reception, but Brielle has no willpower to celebrate anything. Too much has been lost, and all she wants is to be alone.

"Are you sure you don't want to hang out with your friends?" Kerrim asks as they head toward his car. "Or we can go see a movie, or—"

"No." She shakes her head. "I just want to go home, if that's okay."

"Of course, it's okay. When you're grieving, everything is okay. Heck, you can even beat me up if you'd like." He opens the passenger door for her. "In fact, I could kinda get into that." He gives her a devilish grin, and she can't help but smile and snicker.

She climbs into the car. "Okay, for one, I could never hurt you—not even if you liked it."

He makes a faux disappointed frown.

She chuckles. "And two, I really do just need some time. And some sleep."

She hasn't slept in days, even before Sister Agatha... There's too much to worry about. All the stuff with the Zodiacs, Frank's ridiculous incarceration and Bea's panic to fix it. She just wishes she could shut her mind off for a precious few hours so that she could get the sleep needed to handle the stress, the heartache, the hell of it all better.

"Okay." He nods and closes the door, then goes around to get into the driver's seat.

The drive is quick and quiet, and when he drops her off at her house, there's no awkward lingering suggestion he expects her to kiss him goodbye. And that's why she's happy they aren't a thing right now. She's aware that making out with him would give her a few hours of numbed bliss, but that's not enough of a reason to do it. And just one kiss wouldn't be fair, to either of them. Tonight, he's just her friend, and he's being exactly the friend she needs. The one who'll leave her alone without question or expectation.

Bea isn't home. She was too busy talking to lawyers and legal reps to come to the funeral, which Brielle respects and prefers. She'd rather Bea's time be spent making an effort than being there only to show her support.

Brielle doesn't need support. She needs a miracle.

So, she brews herself the strongest sleepy-time tea possible, then climbs into bed after swiftly downing it.

Hours go by, and though her body, heart and soul are bone tired, her mind won't stop long enough to keep her from tossing and turning. She sees Sister Agatha dead under that log. Sees Tristan looking at Ada with hope that she's the one. Sees Frank getting tucked into the police car.

And there's nothing she can do about any of it.

After what has to be the tenth time she's rolled over, the wristwatch Ada gave all the Zodiacs vibrates. She opens her eyes with the greatest reluctance, hoping to see green flashing from it. Green means nothing major. Heck, even orange would mean she can maybe *try* to sleep for a bit longer.

But, just as with everything else in her life, she has no such luck.

The light is red. *Ah, pitch.*

5

ERIC

The breeze wafting off the ocean is crisp, cool, and like a waving hand beckoning them to continue further on the path they've taken.

"I can't believe we just did that!" Eric stares out over the beach, watching the waves crest and fall in perfect rhythm against the backdrop of the slowly setting sun.

Ada's hand finds his, her fingers braiding into his and tangling into the sand as they do so. "I can." Her smile is brilliant, like an LED light bulb outshining the magnificent and jealous sun. "It's about two years overdue, if you ask me."

They've just run away from Chestnut Hill. Never again will they have to parade themselves in front of prospective adoptive parents and pray they don't get separated. Never again will they have to eat the same crappy oatmeal and baloney sandwiches, and sleep on those lumpy mattresses that are too small and smell of mildew.

They're free!

"So…what do we do now?" There's a knot in Eric's gut as he asks the question, but he knows Ada has a plan. She always has a plan. She'll take care of them. And he'll do his best to take care of her.

She sighs, hanging her head on her shoulders as she looks out over the glorious orange and blue horizon, the laughter and play of the beachgoers around them fading into white noise.

"Well, we'll need to get jobs."

He quirks his brow. "Who's going to hire a couple of thirteen-year-olds off the street?"

She shrugs. "Nobody here." She turns to him with a wry smile. "That's why we need to move to a place where they're not afraid to hire under the table."

Eric narrows his eyes. "Where did you have in mind?" They've lived in Philadelphia their whole lives. Where could they go that would be better? And that they could afford?

"The Big Apple, of course."

His eyes bug out. "New York City? You were serious?"

She nods once.

"How are we even going to get there?" he stammers.

"Please." She shrugs again and looks back to the sunset. "I've been pilfering from the donation box for weeks. We have plenty enough for a pair of train tickets and an extremely budget motel room for a few days."

Eric's smile widens as he shakes his head. Just as he thought. Ada always has a plan. "Okay, so we get to NY and rent a motel. Then what?"

"Then I put my elite computer skills to work." She angles her head on one shoulder. "I've been searching Craigslist, and there are a couple gigs I can easily manage. They just need to accept that I'm...younger...which won't pass until we actually get there and they meet me in person. But," she turns to him with a confident smile. "Have no fear. I got us."

"And I've got you. No matter what." He smiles back.

So. New York, here they come.

The alcohol and Molly combo doesn't have a dampening effect on his pain manipulation as Eric approaches the two figures in the darkness. If anything, it amplifies it. The heavier, obviously male figure immediately crumples to the sand, curling into a ball of agony as he shrieks in a very unmanly fashion.

Eric reaches Jenn's frightened silhouette, finally seeing her face in the echoed light of the cantina as he gets within a foot of her.

"Are you alright?" he asks, bracing her shoulders with his strong hands.

She's shaking under his grasp, and though she's clearly scared, her facial features smooth as she puts on a brave face. She swallows and nods. "Yes, but—" She looks down at her assailant, who's still writhing in pain. "Wh—I—he —m—"

"Don't worry about him." Eric tugs her back toward the bar and escorts her to a stool. He looks up at Pablo. "Can you please call her a cab?"

As Jenn sits, she scrunches her brow at Eric in confusion. "What just happened out there? Did you taze him or something?"

The edges of Eric's lip tip up in amusement. "Something like that."

She shakes her head and pushes some stray frazzled hairs away from her face. "Well, whatever you did, I don't know how to thank you. I've been coming down here for years and nothing like that has ever happened." She leans over the bar top and rests her forehead in her hands, trying to calm herself.

"Dangerous people are everywhere, always waiting for their chance to creep out of the shadows." He knows all too well about that. "I'm just glad I was able to step in before he hurt you."

She sits back up and begins to dig around in her purse. "Well, the least I can do is—" She starts to pull out a wad of cash.

Eric presses his hands firmly against hers, stopping her. "No, you really don't have to. Any decent person would've done the same."

"I think you might be the only one left." She laughs nervously. "There must be *something* I can do for you. The offer still stands for you to come back to my hotel with me. You know, to keep me safe." She gives him a flirtatious wink to mask her true desire not to be alone.

Her words almost urge him to accept the invitation. What sort of gentleman would he be if he didn't see her home safely? But he knows it wouldn't end there. He'd end up staying the night.

And that's something he just can't do. Not with the ghost of Ada haunting him, literally.

He sucks in air between his teeth. "As tempting as that is, I can't." Her face tightens in rejection, making his heart clench with guilt. "It's not you. You're beautiful. But I just got dumped pretty hard and I'm not ready for anything physical yet. I hope you don't take it personally."

She frowns, but nods. "Well, whoever she is, she's a fool for letting go of a great guy like you."

The compliment is like a punch to his gut, momentarily knocking the breath from his lungs.

"Senora Yenn, jour taxi's here," Pablo says, pointing to the fresh pair of headlights peeking through the open entrance.

She slides down off her stool a bit shakily. "Thank you, again. And if you need anything while you're here, please don't hesitate to call me. Don't lose my number." She smiles, waves and quickly scampers to the waiting yellow cab as if she's afraid to be in the dark for too long.

"What 'bout jou, senor?" Pablo asks. "Jou wanna cab?"

Eric shakes his head. "No gracias. I could use the walk."

"Okay, but at least take this." Pablo hands him another bottle of water. "On the house!"

Eric nods once as he takes the sweaty bottle. Then, without further ado, he strolls out of the bar as Jenn's cab drives away. His hotel really isn't far.

He looks to his right where he'd left the crippled attacker, but there's no one there. He must have run off as soon as Eric stopped inflicting him with his pain manipulation. Smart move. Eric would've had fun tormenting him further and making sure he never hurt another woman ever again.

With a sigh, he heads out into the night.

After a few minutes, the hairs on the back of his neck begin to tingle, and he can't shake the eerie feeling that someone is behind him. He turns around, but the dirt road is completely void of any figures. Not even a stray dog, of which there's no shortage in this sleepy town.

The Ada hallucinations must be making him paranoid. Or maybe it's the Molly wearing off, leaving him depleted of serotonin.

He shakes it off and continues forward.

As he walks, there's an unmistakable crunch of sand behind him. Soft and light, but repeating.

Footsteps.

He glances over his shoulder without slowing, and again, no one's behind him. At least, not that he can see. A suspicion sneaks into his mind, and he has an idea.

He unscrews the bottle of water and chugs the entire thing. Once it's empty, he feigns a stumble, pretending to be too drunk, and casually tosses it onto the ground at his feet.

One step, two steps, three steps, four.

Scuffle, scuffle.

The bottle goes rattling off to the side of the road.

I knew it. Skins.

Tristan mentioned that they could make themselves invisible somehow. He's not just being paranoid. He's being followed.

As Eric rounds a corner, he kicks into a sprint, running as fast as can toward his hotel. He's spent most of his life running, so he makes it to the towering building in record time.

Once inside the lobby, he backs up against the other side of a wall that conceals him and carefully watches the front door to see if it opens by itself, or if anyone solid and visible walks in. His pounding heart counts the minutes as they pass, and that door doesn't budge.

Maybe he lost them. Or maybe they knew they'd been found so they forfeited the chase.

Either way, he dashes up to his room and begins to pack his meager belongings.

He can't stay here anymore. Time to run again.

6

ADA

The dingy storefront that Ada stands before is just what she expected it to be. Seedy. Dirty. Unclear whether the place is even open for business.

But according to the phone number she called, this is it. She straightens her spine, as if looking taller can help her look older. She told the guy on the phone she's fifteen. She just has to hope that's old enough for the "computer administration" role they're looking for.

And that she doesn't look like the two years younger she really is.

It's a good thing Eric didn't come with her or he'd already be walking away, saying this isn't safe. Not when they need the money.

Not when it was her idea to run away and now they need to find a way to survive.

She pushes open the door. It's glass, but so grimy that she can't see through it. She stops as she enters, her eyes adjusting to the gloom. The place is as seedy and dirty on the inside as it is the outside. A desk is to her left, a computer on it, while a coffee maker she doubts anyone's touched since the turn of the century sits on a bench to her right.

A guy's head appears from behind the computer screen. "Yes?" he asks brusquely.

Ada curls her fingers into her palms, electricity tingling along their tips. She's not going to dial down her defense response until she knows what she's just walked into.

"I'm Ada. I spoke to someone about the computer administration role."

The guy pushes to his feet, and she sees that he's relatively young, maybe seventeen years old. Who knows, maybe he's like her and only sixteen, but pretending to be older.

"Ah, yes." He steps around the desk, his gaze combing her from head to toe. She lifts her chin, getting more and more nervous but having no intention of letting him see that. For some reason, the guy smiles. "Hi, I'm Carlton."

He steps forward, his hand extended and his face smiling. Knowing this is a test, Ada doesn't hesitate as she does the same. She shakes his hand firmly, but releases it as soon as it's polite, hoping he doesn't notice any tingling.

"Nice to meet you, Carlton," she says politely.

He narrows his eyes, although his smile stays in place. "So, you said you're familiar with cryptocurrency and online money management."

Ada nods. The first any amateur computer geek knows of, the second she had no idea what it meant, but intends on being a fast learner. "Yep. I've played around with Bitcoin and most other digital asset types."

Carlton's smile grows. "Great. Let's see what you can do."

He steps back and indicates for Ada to take a seat at the computer. She shuffles past him, noting he's a nice-looking guy, but also conscious that doesn't make him trustworthy.

She shuffles the mouse, quickly getting a sense of the software already uploaded. "What did you want me to do?"

Carlton smiles again. "Our...organization runs several online ventures. Any profits come in as gaming currency, which we then transfer and allocate to various banking institutions."

Ada stills. That lengthy sentence can be distilled into two words.

Money laundering.

She can already see Eric shaking his head as he tells her to get the hell out of here.

Except they need food. Somewhere to live.

If they don't find something, they'll have to go back, and Ada can't stomach the thought of that.

There's nothing she won't do to make sure they stay together.

She glances at the open web browser. "You're using a proxy server? And anonymizing software?"

"We sure are. Just open the folder labeled Cancelled Orders."

Ada does as she's told, well aware she's getting herself involved in something deeply illegal. She dabbled in this stuff at the orphanage—it was the only way to search what she and Eric can do without a trace. But this is next level stuff. It has her heart thudding and she has to stop her leg from jiggling beneath the table.

She can't afford to look nervous. Nor can she afford to get too worked up...

A password protected site opens and she looks up at Carlton. "So there's essentially no IP address?"

His smile impossibly grows some more. "Essentially." His gaze sharpens. "We need someone who's willing to do what it takes without asking too many questions."

Ada pushes to her feet, knowing she has a decision to make.

This is dangerous. She's being asked to step on the other

side of the law.

But… she could learn to be even more untraceable. She and Eric could almost completely disappear off the grid.

She shrugs. "You don't ask any questions of me, I won't ask any of you."

Carlton lets out a short laugh. "I like you, Ada. I suspect we're going to become fast friends."

Tristan entering HQ snaps Ada out of her musings.

That day feels like a lifetime ago. She and Eric were so excited.

Even then, she hid the truth from Eric. She thought it was justified because she was doing it for them. Everything she's ever done has been for them, but she screwed up.

She needs to find him.

She has to make this right.

Tristan rubs his mussed hair, Jareth not far behind him. "What's up?"

"Dark matter disturbance," she says, getting straight to the point. "In three locations."

Logan and Cassandra enter just as she finishes the sentence. Their faces light up in the same way Tristan's does.

"Could it be another Zodiac?" Cassandra asks excitedly.

"Maybe." But one of them is Eric, she's sure of it. "But it could also be Skins."

"Skins?" Brielle asks sharply, pausing as she enters. "Where?"

"Excellent," comes Esther's calm voice through the speakers. "Everyone's here. I've detected dark matter disturbances in three locations. Berlin, Roosevelt Island, and Rocky Point."

The Zodiacs all glance at each other, variations of the

same apprehension and anticipation Ada's been feeling shifting across their faces.

"I'm unable to identify what has triggered the changes," Esther continues. "There's no way to tell whether it's another Zodiac or Skins."

Except Ada knows what one of them is. She knows where Eric's gone.

Tristan frowns. "We'll need to split up. Investigate each location."

"Absolutely," Esther responds. "And I've already calculated the best pairing of Zodiacs."

He glances at Ada with raised brows and she shrugs sheepishly. She hadn't intended for Esther to be quite so bossy.

"And how did you come up with this, Esther?" he asks dryly.

"Multiple factors were entered into the algorithm, Tristan. Fighting expertise. Length of time as a Zodiac. Personal variables."

Ada's gaze slinks away from Tristan as she tries not to flush. Trying to quantify the ongoing awkwardness between Tristan and Brielle wasn't easy. Just like trying to quantify the yearning to find Eric was impossible. Even the largest number in the world, googolplex, can't capture the ache that's clawing at her very soul.

"Tristan and Jareth, you'll investigate Roosevelt Island."

He nods, his gaze flickering to Brielle and away. "Makes sense."

"And Brielle and Cassandra, you investigate Berlin. Your powers are quite complementary."

Cassandra seems to hesitate, no doubt reluctant to be away from Logan, but also recognizing that someone with offensive powers needs to go with Brielle.

"And Logan, you and Ada investigate Rocky Point," says

Esther. "Ada, you may need Logan's calming powers as you work to get your powers under control."

Ada would hug Esther if she could. She knows just like Ada does that Eric's in Rocky Point. He always spoke of going to Mexico thanks to his love of Mexican food.

And yes, Logan's ability to calm emotions might be needed when she finally finds Eric.

He's going to be hurt. And angry.

But she needs him to listen to her.

Tristan glances around the room. "Everyone happy with that?"

Cassandra crosses her arms, huffing. "Next time, I'm going to help with those algorithms."

Logan nods. "It makes sense this time around," he agrees, glancing at Cassandra. It's clear he wishes they'd been paired up just as much as she does.

"Okay," says Tristan. "Let's roll out."

"I'll meet you at the car," says Jareth and he lifts his cell to his ear, no doubt to ring Veronica and tell her what's going on.

Cassandra glances at Brielle. "We need to pack."

Brielle nods. "And book flights."

"There are ample funds in the Zodiac account," says Esther.

Tristan nods. He told Ada that Zarius and Tess made sure he and the others would always have the means they need to fulfil their quest.

The girls nod, Brielle heading to the exit. Cassandra goes to follow, only to quickly dart to Logan. She plants a kiss so passionate on his lips that everyone in the room looks away.

Brielle pauses as she passes Ada. "Good luck," she says softly.

Ada stills. They haven't spoken about it, but they knew each other before all this. Does Brielle remember Carlton?

"Thanks. You, too."

Brielle's smile is small but there, nonetheless. It has Ada wishing there was more time to talk.

But Logan appears beside her. "You packed?"

She nods. "I have a bag ready." She's been prepared for this from the moment Eric walked out of her life.

"Me, too," he says with an impressed grin. "Just in case."

Ada lifts her clenched hand and they fist bump. "Let's do this."

They head up the stairs, not far behind Cassandra and Brielle. She notes Tristan's light footsteps quickly catching up.

Ada's conscious that each of the Zodiacs are leaving, preparing to leave for their destination under the cover of night.

None of them knowing what they're going to find.

7

TRISTAN

The longer the bus trundles down the suburban streets of New York, the more restless Tristan becomes. He should've stayed at the motel and waited until Zarius and Tess went out. Then he could've searched for the book and read it for himself. He's twelve—old enough to be trusted with this stuff.

He shoots to his feet and presses the button, energy buzzing through his muscles. The bus jerks right and Tristan sees that they were just coming up to a stop. The driver must've assumed he almost missed it. Tristan stumbles but quickly makes his way to the doors. He has no idea where he is, but that doesn't really bother him. He barely pays attention to what city or town or state they're in anymore.

The only place that will ever register on his radar is one where he finds a Zodiac Heir.

"Thanks," he mumbles over his shoulder as he descends the steps.

As the bus rumbles away, Tristan finds himself on a downtown street like countless others he's seen. He realizes he's now going to have to wait for a bus to come the other way and take him back to the motel.

Great.

Deciding to work off some of the restless energy while he waits, Tristan jams his hands in his pockets and sets off. He'll do some laps of the block while he kills time. The jumble of people around him look just like him—heads down, gazes unfocused yet wary at the same time. Everyone's keeping to themselves as they get to wherever they're going, but still on alert, as if a mugging is only a blink away.

The corner of the block is ahead, and Tristan decides to go left purely because he can smell a bakery in that direction. He may as well get something good out of this temper tantrum that now has him walking through who-knows-what suburb in New York.

A man in a business suit in front of him suddenly stops, and Tristan quickly side steps.

"Oh, sorry," says a teen as he crashes into the man, bounding off and righting himself.

"Watch where you're going, kid," the man growls.

The red-haired, freckle faced teen rolls his eyes before walking away, taking a sharp right into an alley.

With the guy's wallet.

The man never registered the pickpocket, but Tristan certainly saw it. He frowns, increasing his pace as he follows. The dude was rude, but that doesn't mean it's okay to steal his money and credit cards.

Although he shouldn't be, Tristan's surprised to find the teen is almost at the other end of the alley, running. He doesn't call out, knowing it'll only alarm him more, instead breaking into a run himself.

The teen disappears around a corner, and Tristan injects more speed. He rounds the corner, seeing another alley, but this time it's empty.

Pitch. He's going to lose him.

Another burst of speed, and he's down the end. It opens out into a dingier part of New York, as if the shortcut just sliced through about three tax brackets of income. Up ahead, Tristan sees the red-haired teen disappear into what looks like an abandoned building. He crosses the road, no longer running.

Conscious he has no idea what he's walking into.

He's now in a more dangerous part of the city, following a thief.

Approaching the doorway lacking a door, he keeps his senses on high alert. He can hear voices inside, several of them, all sounding relatively young.

Suddenly, the red-haired teen appears in front of Tristan, making him rear back. "Hey, no need to knock. We have an open-door policy." He grins, indicating to the nonexistent door. "Get it? An open-door policy?"

"Ah, yeah, I get it," says Tristan, not quite sure what to make of the smiling guy in front of him. The one who's a pickpocket.

"Hi," he says. "My name's Malachi."

"Hey, I'm Tristan." He glances past Malachi, trying to get a sense of what he's stumbled upon. A nest of friendly-faced thieves who are going to roll him the minute he turns his back? Or just a bunch of homeless kids who will just let anyone through their door?

"We've got another one," Malachi calls over his shoulder.

"Another one, what?" Tristan asks.

Malachi turns back, his smile still in place. "Another curious kid from the burbs who wants to see how the other half lives."

Tristan frowns but doesn't bother to correct Malachi. He's lived in everything from a dingy hotel to a penthouse apartment, depending on what Zarius and Tess can find that will take their fake IDs without too much question.

"I saw you—"

A kid jumps up from where he was squatting down, holding what looks like a bill in his hand. "Twenty bucks!" he shouts triumphantly.

Malachi spins around, walking toward the group. "Great! We should be able to get Jay something nice."

Tristan follows, still trying to get a sense of what's going on. He sees the man's wallet lying on the ground, credit cards and driver's license still in it. The four or five kids are far more excited that they've found cash.

A quick look around and his eyebrows hike up. The internal walls of the dilapidated building are covered in graffiti, not dirty tags and illegible scribbles, but some of the best artwork he's ever seen. Powerful colors and sweeping strokes create a haphazard mural that stretches from one end of the vast room to another. There are smiling cartoon faces with big noses and daisies the size of a person and a burning phoenix that takes his breath away.

"Pretty good, huh?" Malachi beams.

"Yeah, it is," Tristan says, impressed. The inside of the building doesn't look old and broken, it looks...alive.

"I did some of it," Malachi says proudly, "But most of it was by our friend, Jay."

"Who got arrested," scowls a dark-haired kid as he comes to stand beside Malachi. He spits onto the concrete floor. "Freaking pigs. Jay wasn't hurtin' no one."

"Yeah, but it's not the first time he's been caught," Malachi says heavily. "This would be the first time he's got a taste of the inside. We need to look after him."

The kid grins. "And twenty bucks should do it."

"It definitely will," beams Malachi. "Let's go get some tacos."

There are several whoops and the bunch of kids stream past Tristan, most barely even looking at him.

Malachi pauses as he passes him. "The other one like you has got himself in a spot of trouble."

Tristan frowns. "I doubt he's anything like me."

Malachi shrugs and follows the others. "You want a burrito?"

Tristan knows he has a bus to catch and book to search for, but something has him trailing the motley bunch. He's spent all his life watching and waiting, never staying long enough in one place to form any sort of connection. He's curious about this ragtag group who seem to be on a crusade of some sort, off to save a talented graffiti artist.

The taco stand is at the end of the block, and Malachi buys as many as he can with the twenty dollar note. He disperses most of them among the kids and teens, keeping three to himself.

"Hey," he calls to Tristan, who's standing at the edge of the group. "Catch."

He throws a foil wrapped taco and Tristan catches it. His stomach clenches as the scent of Mexican spices hits his nostrils and he realizes he's hungry.

"Ah, thanks," he says, lifting the taco to acknowledge Malachi.

Malachi grins. "We all look out for each other."

They're a team. A family.

A pang of envy stabs Tristan in the gut. Will they ever find enough Zodiacs to be able to do the same?

The group keeps moving, and Tristan's footsteps falter when he realizes where these kids are going. Something he would've figured out if he let himself think for longer than a second.

Mirror Point Police Department is stamped across the top of the square, brick building in bold white letters.

Tristan takes a step back. Zarius's voice jolts through his mind.

Stay off the police radar. Never bring attention to yourself.

Malachi turns around, his eyebrows rising. "Ah, so you're more like us than I thought."

"I'm not here for any trouble," says Tristan in a low voice. He shouldn't have come here. He should've just waited to get the first bus back to the motel.

"Neither am I," says Malachi. "I'm just helping out a friend."

"Which is heartwarming, but it's not my fight."

Malachi looks at him for long seconds. "Except you followed us here," he points out.

Tristan's shoulders bunch up, not liking that Malachi's pointed that out. "Whoever this Jay is, I'm glad someone's got his back." Maybe one day, Tristan will have that, too. "He seems very talented. But I'm not the one who can help him."

"Actually, Jay's not his real name. It's—"

"What is the meaning of all this?"

Tristan tenses as he sees a grizzled cop standing outside the door, his hand casually resting on his firearm. His narrowed gaze takes in the dozen or so group of dirty, baggy clothed teens.

With a clean-faced Tristan at the back with his neatly pressed t-shirt because Tess insists on ironing everything, saying she won't have him looking like he lives out of a suitcase. Even though he lives out of a suitcase...

Tristan spins on his heel. He can't be here for this.

Long strides take him away from the group as someone shouts back at the cop, probably the precinct captain, that they're here to see Jay. The cop says something back, but Tristan doesn't try to hear. The less he knows about what's going on here, the better.

He's just turned a corner when a suited man steps in front of him. He flashes a silver badge.

"Agent Cadbury, Jack Cadbury. FBI. I'd like to have a word."

The frowning, balding face of Jack jolts Tristan out of the memory. He's chosen not to think about that day, purely because it was the first time he ran into the FBI agent. It was one he'd preferred to have forgotten.

But as he waits in the garage for Jareth, it reminds him he'd been to New York before. Briefly, and they'd run like hell afterward, but they had most definitely been here.

And crossing paths with a talented graffiti artist couldn't have been a coincidence.

Jareth arrives, a duffel bag over his shoulder that he throws into the back, alongside Tristan's. Just like Ada and Logan, he has one packed and ready for moments like these.

They climb in but Tristan pauses behind the steering wheel. "Did you ever meet a guy called Malachi?"

Jareth's brow spikes up. "Yeah. He looked after me when I, well, rebelled." He shrugs. "I had these…skills I didn't know what to do with." His gaze sharpens. "Why?"

"I was here in New York when I was thirteen. We didn't stay longer than a day. It was so brief that I don't think I even registered the name of the suburb."

Jareth's jaw drops a little. "It was Roosevelt Island."

Tristan swallows, not entirely sure what this means. "I ran into a kid called Malachi. He was helping out a kid called Jay."

"The name I used when I was on the streets," Jareth says, looking stunned. He frowns. "Last I heard Malachi was shot. Gang violence."

Sadness jolts through Tristan. "I'm sorry to hear that. He seemed like a nice guy." Someone who cared about the kids living on the streets.

"Yeah, he was. He was the one who convinced me to go back home." Jareth's eyes widen. "And it was someone called Dyad who wiped my record clean."

Shock has Tristan rooted to the leather seat.

It seems the Zodiacs were crossing paths long before any of them realized.

He turns the keys in the ignition, wishing there was time to figure out what it all means. But Ada's new technology means they've taken their search to the next level.

There's a disturbance in dark matter they have to investigate.

And he's hoping with everything he has that it's another Zodiac Guardian.

8

BRIELLE

Brielle's so excited! Carlton's visited her at the orphanage several times over the last few weeks, and today he's taking her out for ice cream. She's on her way to the ice cream shop now to meet him, pedaling as fast as her bike will go.

He's sitting at a stone table outside the shop when she rolls up, and when he sees her, a smile blooms across his cute face. It makes Brielle feel special, like she has a true friend again. It makes the sting of Cassandra's hatred a little less piercing.

She hops off the bike and leans it up against the wall before joining him.

"Hey, I'm glad you could make it." His smile makes her heart flutter. "It's nice seeing you away from the orphanage for a change."

"Yeah, thanks for inviting me. I never really have an excuse to leave." Feeling instantly stupid for saying that, she lets slip a nervous giggle. She doesn't want him to know that she's a social outcast.

"What'll you have?" He gestures to the wall of the shop

and the pictures of the various ice creams and popsicles they offer.

"Oh, er, nothing for me." She waves her hand.

He raises an eyebrow. "Why not?"

She looks down at her fingers fiddling with each other on top of the stone table. "I don't have any money."

"Duh," he says. "I knew that when I invited you. Obviously, I'm paying for you."

Her cheeks burn. "Oh." The offer is so nice, she can't possibly reject it. She glances at the wall and picks the first popsicle she sees. "I'll have a strawberry shortcake pop."

Nodding once, he turns and goes to the order window. Now that his back is turned, she runs her hands over her face. Why did she do that? She doesn't even like strawberry! But Carlton is so cute and so nice, her brain goes to mush around him. Figures the one time someone offers to buy her ice cream, she's too dazed and foolish to order something she actually likes.

She recovers just in time for him to return with their treats in hand. He passes her the plastic-wrapped concoction, then tears into his own. A fudgesicle. His eyes widen with eagerness at the sight of it, just before he opens his mouth and takes a big bite.

He looks at her expectantly as he savors the chocolatey goodness, so she unwraps hers and takes a modest nibble. The softened cookie crumbles on the outside are sweet, tolerable, but the ice cream underneath is still strawberry. She smiles as she chews to mask her displeasure.

Once she reluctantly swallows, she opens her mouth to thank him.

"Hey, Carlton," says an unfamiliar female voice behind her.

As Brielle begins to turn, an older girl, closer to Carlton's age, comes into view at the end of the table. She's pretty, and the mass of bright orange curls that frame her face makes her look even prettier. Is she his girlfriend? Brielle can't help the twist of jealousy coiling within her.

"Hey, Ada." Carlton sets his fudgesicle back onto the wrapper and stands. "Did you bring it?"

Ada's green eyes flicker to Brielle, as if Brielle is the one invading their conversation. "Yes."

"Great." Carlton smiles that hundred watt smile. "Would you like a popsicle, too? My treat?" He points his thumb at the order window.

"Oh. Uh, sure, I guess." Ada seems to feel out of place, and she hardly regards Brielle anymore. "I'll take a rocket pop."

He darts back to the window to get her order, and Ada finally decides to sit at the very edge of the stone bench farthest from Brielle.

Never a big fan of awkward silences, Brielle attempts to break the ice. "How do you know Carlton? Do you go to the same school?"

Ada turns to look at her, and Brielle's vision begins to tunnel and spiral.

Oh no. Not here, not now!

Brielle is thrust into a vision. It's blurry and confusing, a clash of flashing images between the face of a cute blond boy and Carlton's face, and the sense of sharp guilt that she's doing something that will hurt the blond guy.

When the vision releases her, Brielle grips the table for support, aware that Ada is looking at her strangely. Brielle clearly missed whatever she'd said during the vision, and all she knows is she has to voice her thoughts or the guilt will never go away.

"You shouldn't do this," Brielle whispers.

Ada's brows push together. "What are you talking about?"

Brielle steals a glance at Carlton, then turns back to Ada. "Whatever you're doing with Carlton..." She can't finish the warning. Mostly because she doesn't even know what Ada's doing with Carlton. She can only surmise from the confusing vision that Ada's cheating on her boyfriend with him.

The realization stabs disappointment into Brielle's gut. So Carlton doesn't like her like that. Of course, why would he? He's older and not an orphan. He's just taking pity on her.

Ada leans closer, her green eyes narrowed venomously. "Why don't you mind your own business? I don't answer to anyone, least of all some goody-two-shoes like you. And if you were as smart as you think you are, you'd stay away from Carlton."

The rebuke is like a slap in the face, and Brielle is too stunned to say or do anything more than sit there with her mouth open.

"Here you go, Ada." Carlton returns and hands Ada the popsicle. As she opens it, he watches her intently, almost anxiously, only confirming Brielle's suspicion.

"Hey, sorry, I forgot there's somewhere I need to be." Brielle rises and climbs over the bench. "See ya later, maybe." She rushes away as he calls after her, only tossing the unwanted strawberry shortcake into a dumpster once he can no longer see her.

She really doesn't fit in anywhere. Maybe she never will.

Staring down at the bracelet Carlton had given her all those years ago as she waits in the airport, Brielle wonders if Ada remembers that first encounter. She hadn't realized right away who Ada was when they met Dyad the first time, only knew she recognized her, and Ada seemed to, too. It was only a few days later that the connection announced itself.

The airport is a bustle of voices and movement as passengers rush to and fro around her, but Brielle's deaf to them, lost in thought. She doesn't know how to feel about Ada. This whole thing between her and Eric seems like a broken record. Did Eric know this wasn't the first time his relationship with Ada had been threatened? Did he know that she'd cheated on him back then with Carlton?

Ada claims to love Eric so much, but how could she truly if she was willing to cheat on him? Of course, Ada must've been fourteen or so at the time, young and foolish. Could she have changed much since then?

A pair of stiletto-covered feet stop in front of her. "Our flight is finally boarding."

Brielle looks up at Cassandra, who's carting around two large rolling suitcases and lugging a heavy duffle bag over her shoulder.

"Did you really need to bring all that?"

Cassandra gives Brielle a look that says "how could you ask me that?" "We have no idea how long we'll be in D.C., and I want to be prepared for every eventuality."

A few days ago, Cassandra returned to her parents' house only to grab her clothes and personal belongings—apparently she'd gotten tired of trying to fit into Brielle's clothes that were too small for her. She's been pretty much living out of those suitcases the last couple days in Brielle's room, and apparently deemed it necessary to bring it all with them now.

Brielle smirks and shakes her head.

"What?" Cassandra asks.

"I'm just glad we're friends again." Brielle gets up off the chair she'd been waiting in. "Let's get on that plane."

She has no idea what awaits them in D.C., but at least she'll have her oldest friend fighting alongside her for whatever they find.

9

ERIC

Eric wanders back into the place they've been calling home for the past couple weeks—an abandoned duplex that's now inhabited by the homeless and runaway teens of New York on the outskirts of the city. Part of a housing development that never got finished.

"Howdy, Eric," calls Malachi, the freckles on his nose lighting up as he smiles at Eric. "Where's your Siamese twin?"

There'd been a running joke with his fellow strays that he and Ada were attached at the hip, because nobody ever saw one without the other.

Eric has to admit, he does feel strangely lacking entering the dingy space without her. Even though he's in good company, it's not *great* company. Not the *ultimate* company.

"She's off at her new 'job.'" He flares both index and middle fingers in air quotes.

He still has no idea what it actually is. She said it was in computing for a small company that pays under the table, and that should've been enough for him, but...he can't help but feel like she's keeping something from him.

"Well, good for her." Malachi salutes with his open soda can, then goes back to work counting change.

Eric is suddenly struck by the new artwork on the wall.

For the last couple weeks, this particular wall had been covered in a very detailed mural of cartoon lilies dancing around in a new school style. Eric had sort of assumed it had always been there. But tonight, the wall has been completely replaced by a vibrant and angry sunset, so powerful it stirs something deep within Eric's chest. The sky almost looks as if it's weeping.

"Uh… What happened to the wall?" He points with what he knows must be a stupid expression on his face.

Malachi turns toward the mural. "Oh… That's Jay."

"What?" Who's Jay? If he's a fellow runaway, Eric hasn't heard of him the last two weeks they've been staying here.

A sudden look of understanding crosses Malachi's face. "Oh right, you haven't met him yet. Umm, he's not like you and I. Not like any of us really. He's not exactly a runaway. He has actual parents. But he likes to do street art. He was in earlier today and made this, and then after…" Malachi's youthful face hardens, revealing the struggles he's lived through. "He got arrested for… being in the wrong place at the wrong time. So a bunch of us are putting together some cash to get him out. We already brought him some munchies, but it's not enough. This is his third strike. If we can't get him out, he'll go to juvie." Malachi grimaces.

It's obvious he cares about this kid that Eric has never met, and because Malachi cares, Eric does, too. Malachi took them in when they had nothing. He and Ada would be living on the streets right now if it weren't for Malachi finding them and offering them shelter, albeit a very unconventional one.

"Hey guys, what's with the long faces?" Ada's cheery voice brightens the suddenly dark room.

"Malachi was just telling me about a fellow lost child in need of help," Eric says. "He painted this mural"—he points to the wall—"and apparently loads of others around town, and he got arrested for his art."

"We need to find a way to get him out before they send him to juvie," Malachi adds.

"It's his third strike," Eric interjects.

Maybe it's the look of enthusiasm on Eric's face, or just her natural desire to help anyone in need, but Ada smiles wide and says, "I can help with that," her emerald eyes twinkling with a spark of mischief.

Malachi lights up. "Really?"

She nods eagerly and comes to sit beside their host, propping open her laptop and beginning to type away like mad. "It's his third strike, you say?"

Malachi hums in affirmation.

"Okay, all it takes is clearing his slate before the case can go before a judge," she says, fingers still typing wildly. "If there are no other strikes on file, there's no case. And he can go free." *Type, type, type.* "Aaaaaand, voila! Problem solved." She sits back, folding her fingers over her flat belly and smirking smugly.

Malachi's jaw drops, eyes wide. "What? Just like that?"

She nods with a huge grin. "Yep. He should be released within the hour."

Malachi's eyes dart from side to side frantically. "Oh my —this is *huge!* I have to get there before he's released! Thank you, Ada. You're incredible!"

Ada shrugs, smiling even wider. "Well…"

Just then, Malachi darts out of the building, and Eric and Ada are left alone in the makeshift living room.

Suddenly, Eric doesn't care what Ada's hiding from him. He knows he can be overprotective, and he trusts that whatever she's up to, she's trying to keep him from a meltdown. Either way, she's taking care of them—of *all* of them.

He closes his arms around her.

"Malachi's right. You're incredible."

"No," she grins. "Dyad is incredible. We now have a codename."

Eric's not sure why it's that particular memory that plays over and over in his mind like a broken record as he descends the staircase and waits for the taxi he hailed under an assumed name.

Maybe it's his subconscious reminding him that Ada has a good heart. That she always has. That day so many years ago, she risked her own safety without question to help some stranger in need *just because* he was in need. And that wasn't the only example of an instance in which she'd done that.

He's angry at her, absolutely. Molten lava angry that she chose Tristan—some stranger who claimed to be her soulmate—over him. But, as he runs for his life away from invisible assassins, he's never felt more lost without her.

The memory of the one called Brielle's sudden disappearance crosses his mind as he taps his fingers impatiently on the counter. Unlike the others who'd been present at the whole gem show thing, Eric had been watching her—everyone for that matter. And he'd seen the shattered expression that broke her pretty face before she took off. Eric would guess that she'd had the hots for Tristan and was just as crushed by the news as Eric was.

No, that's not right. No one could ever compare to the level of tortured existence he now finds himself in. But it must have been similar.

The point is, there are a handful of other Zodiacs who

would understand his plight, that he could lean on in situations like this, even if he does have to watch Ada fawn over Tristan the rest of his life.

Can he do that? Can he sacrifice his heart and emotional sanity for the sake of having a team to rely on and work with? Or is he willing to spend his life on the run from invisible beings who want only to kill him and bury him in the desert where his body will never be found…

Not for the first time, he truly wonders how long he can survive without seeing Ada's face. Apparently, his drug battered brain has answered that for him, as it's manifesting her ghost everywhere he turns.

"How are you going to outsmart them?"

Eric jumps with a quickly muffled shout at her sudden appearance on the counter beside him, perched just as she was in the bar.

"Shh," he hisses harshly. "I don't want them to hear." He realizes she's a figment of his imagination, so he should be able to answer her with his thoughts. And he does.

"Ah, clever." She tilts her pretty head. "Hope it works. Don't go dying on me."

He rolls his eyes. "Like you care," he mutters.

Her heart-shaped face looks pained for a moment. She leans forward on the counter, closer to him. "Of course, I do. You know I do. That's why I'm here."

"But you're not!" he snaps, then instantly remembers to lower his voice.

Besides, he's done talking to her. Never mind that her make-believe presence is a comfort, but the conversation is going to get him killed.

"Gotcha," she says with a wink, running her fingers across her lips in a zipper motion.

Mercifully, his burner phone buzzes in his hands, illuminating with a message that lets him know the taxi is waiting out by the side entrance, just as he requested. Bundling a white sheet around himself like he's some stray Arabian dignitary, he rushes out the side door and hops into the style running cab.

"Where to, senor?" the driver asks in the front.

"Airport. As fast as you can."

"Jou got it!" The driver almost lazily turns in a circle in the parking lot and pulls onto the road.

"I said as fast as you can," Eric prompts.

"Ah yes, but la policia is out this time of night, necessito be careful, jou know," he says in broken English as he cranks the wheel.

"Mm-hmm," Eric hums and tries to relax in the back seat.

The cab moves leisurely through the sleepy roads of Cholla Bay, but as promised, as soon as they get onto the straight away, the car begins to accelerate.

Throughout their escape from the small beach suburb, Eric had been looking out the back window, making sure they hadn't been followed, and there were no car lights behind them. But as they turn onto the straight, when he looks back this time, car lights flash on only a car length behind them.

"Huh, es extrano," the driver says, glancing at his side mirror.

Eric doesn't know the words, but he guesses by the context that he's saying something like, "what the hell?"

Eric leans forward and slaps his hand on the chair in front him. "Go faster!"

"No necesito, señor." The driver waves his hand. "Pro'ly just cartel trying to stay hidden. We just let them pass."

Eric pulse spikes. No way in Hell is that just cartel. It's Skins.

"Trust me, you have to go faster. Now!"

"Hondale," the driver sighs, shaking his head, but the speedometer doesn't change.

"I'm serious!" Eric is shouting at this point. "If you don't speed up, we'll both be in major trouble."

"Sientate, muchacho, or I pull over!" the driver shouts, pointing his index finger at Eric.

Suddenly, the cab is jarred roughly from the left side, nearly knocking Eric over on the back bench.

"Chinga!" the driver shouts as he yanks on the steering wheel to right the vehicle.

But just as he does, another smack rocks them from the right.

They're surrounded!

"Brake!" Eric roars, gripping the driver's seat with both hands.

"Que?" The driver seems too preoccupied with the current situation to bother with an attempt at translation.

Eric's mind races for the Spanish word but finds none. "Stop!"

Too late, red lights flash in front of them as they smash into the back of a third vehicle.

For a handful of seconds that feel like an hour, Eric sluggishly peels himself off the back of the driver's seat, his ears ringing so loud he's convinced that's all his existence has been reduced to. With each achingly slow second, he becomes more aware of his situation.

The driver is slumped over the steering wheel, no airbags deployed—probably took them out—and blood drips down the wheel as his eyes stare blankly into nothing.

The sound of doors opening and slamming propel Eric into action, but with the sudden crash he just experienced and the loss of orientation that resulted, he just about falls onto the sand when he opens the door.

The Skins materialize from the darkness as they

approach him, their shadowed faces grinning wickedly in the faint red glow of the various brake lights. Eric jumps to his feet, stumbling a bit. Luckily, he doesn't need to be physically up to par to fight back.

Conjuring his power, he radiates pain with every conscious fiber of his being, and the dozen or so men and women around him visibly crumple, crying out as they fall.

Still concentrating, Eric tries to focus through the piercing ring in his head. He needs to get into one of these cars. If he can get a good head start, inflicting pain until it can't reach them anymore, he might be able to get away.

He takes a step and stumbles, catching himself as he nearly faceplants the sand. He doesn't have much faith in his ability to both drive and continue to inflict pain, but it's his only shot. He *needs* to get into one of these vehicles!

Confusingly, a pair of small hands grips his shoulders. Panic-stricken, he revolts, twisting all about to swat at the hands. He's not surprised to see Ada's green eyes glowing in the darkness.

"Leave me be!" he groans, waving her away as he continues to make his way toward an open sedan.

"Eric, you have to come with us *now!*" her voice booms.

Wait, us?

In a glance, he spots a somewhat familiar buff man not far behind her. A name pops into his head. *Logan.*

His brain slowly calculates what's happening. If this were a hallucination, it would be Tristan with her, not this insignificant Zodiac he barely remembers. She's not a figment of his imagination. This Ada is *real!*

"Hurry up!" she pleads, yanking on his arm. "Before they come to."

Eric doesn't hesitate. He jettisons into gear, allowing his ex and her companion to push him into a fourth vehicle as he puts all his concentration on keeping the Skins incapacitated.

The vehicle beneath them roars as it speeds down the road, and within seconds, Eric feels when the connection is severed, when he can no longer reach the Skins with his powers. Soon they'll spring back to life and continue on the chase.

But Logan has driven so swiftly, so tactfully around corners and alleyways, they'd need a miracle to find them now.

Eric gapes at the very real, solid form of Ada sitting beside him in the backseat. His mind blares the question he can't voice—"What are you doing here?"

"We're rescuing you, obviously," she answers, apparently still able to read his mind. She shakes her head, as if the question he *didn't ask* was a stupid one.

He finds his voice enough to ask, "How did you find me?"

Turning her head away from its watchful post in the rear window, her face softens as she looks at him. "Esther flagged three spikes in dark matter. When Rocky Point was one of them, I knew that had to be you." She looks down at her lap and blushes, not a bright red, but a sad pink. "You always mentioned how you'd love to go to Mexico one day. And Rocky Point is the ideal place for someone to try to get lost."

He grinds his teeth at how well she still knows him, but he can't help but feel grateful for her sudden arrival just when he needed it. She has a knack for doing that.

He rubs his head, which still throbs with a dull ache from the collision—and admittedly also from the copious amounts of alcohol he's had. "Where are we going?"

She looks at him with a warm but pleading smile. "Home?" The end of her voice sounds like a question, and even now, he hates hearing the pained doubt in her voice. She hangs her head and sighs, which turns into a long-suffering groan.

"I have a lot to explain to you."

ADA

Ada sits on the bench seat beside the park, tapping away on the laptop resting on her thighs. The sun hits her back, warming it, and she angles the screen so she's shading it, watching as the hourglass icon twirls.

"Come on, come on," she says under her breath.

Transfer successful.

"Yes," she hisses, quickly looking around as she says it louder than intended. But the elderly couple power walking past are both wearing headphones, and the mother with the twin stroller is most definitely preoccupied.

They're all clueless to the money laundering happening only a few feet away.

Ada curls back into the bench, a mix of uneasiness and triumph churning through her gut. Her transactions are going more and more underground, using digital currencies, anonymous shell accounts, and iframes. She's earning steady money. But it's highly illegal.

And wrong.

"Hey there, gorgeous. I've been looking for you." She

looks up, finding Carlton standing above her. "Not a fan of the office, huh?"

Ada wrinkles her nose. "Bad lighting."

Not to mention she has no desire to be connected to that building if it ever gets raided, even if they're using a VPN to hide their IP address.

Carlton sits beside her, smiling. "Yeah, shady office for shady dealings."

Ada doesn't say anything, the uneasiness growing. Carlton's always been far more comfortable with this than her. "Just getting vitamin D," she says lightly.

"Whilst doing the shady dealings?" he asks with a wink.

Her shoulders tighten. "Yep. Just finished another transfer. There's no way anyone will track it back to the original source."

Carlton's eyes warm. "You're a natural."

She tries to smile, she really does, but there's no way that's a compliment. She's doing this so she and Eric can have money to eat. Maybe somewhere to live that's not an abandoned building. It's a necessity.

His gaze turns thoughtful as he leans in closer. "You okay? Is there anything you want to talk about?"

For the briefest of seconds, Ada's tempted. She's tempted to tell him why she ran away from the orphanage. That she can do things no one else can. Carlton has been nothing but helpful and caring. But she bites her lip. This isn't just her secret, it's Eric's too.

Instead, she asks him something else that's been bothering her. "Who was that girl? The one at the ice cream shop."

His eyebrows shoot up. "Her? Just some girl who looked like she needed a friend and an ice cream. I was just being friendly." He angles his head, the light glinting off his teasing gaze. "Why? You jealous?"

Ada jolts, realizing how close Carlton is. She shuffles back a little. "No, I think it's great that you're helping other girls." Girls like her.

For the first time, she wonders what Carlton's motivation is. She assumed with her it was her computer skills that drew him in. But the other girl seemed far more vulnerable. More impressionable.

You shouldn't do this.

And yet, the girl knew what Ada's doing. She knew about the hacking and money laundering. Ada frowns. There's a link here that she's missing.

Carlton leans away, his easy smile back. "Sure. Just trying to help." He shrugs. "She looked like she needed someone to talk to."

Ada relaxes, deciding she's read this wrong. "And I'm sure she appreciates it as much as I do."

He looks up, his face full of boyish charm. "Thanks, Ada." Just as the moment is stretching a little too long, he pushes to his feet. "I'd better go. I'll see you back at the office?"

"Sure thing," she says, waving as he walks away, wishing the uneasiness would go away.

Her hand pauses midair.

Someone else is at the park. Standing beside a tree.

Eric.

And he looks stricken.

Ada jumps to her feet, clutching her computer as she rushes to him. "Eric, what are you doing here?"

He lifts a foil wrapped hotdog. "I brought you some lunch," he says, his voice hollow. "I didn't realize you had company."

She glances over her shoulder, seeing that Carlton's gone. "You remember Carlton. He's the one who offered me the job."

"He sure seems…friendly."

Ada jolts. Eric's jealous? "He's been really helpful, but it's nothing more than that."

"He's interested in you, Ada. I can feel it." He clenches his jaw. "I could see it."

She presses a hand to his arm, feeling the tension practically vibrating through him. "It doesn't matter what he thinks." She pulls in a trembling breath. She's never said the words, but she's wanted to. Maybe now's the time. "I l—"

Eric takes a step back. "I thought we were in this together."

Ada opens her mouth to object, to tell him he's the other half of her soul, but Eric strides away. He doesn't look back, his spine looking far too tense and unyielding even if he wanted to.

Her shoulders sag. Can't he see she's doing it for them?

They're at the airport before Ada finally has a chance alone with Eric. Logan glances between them before saying he's going to get them something to eat, leaving them near the gate. Ada nods, even though the last thing her churning stomach wants is food.

Eric's been silent and withdrawn the whole drive here. Barely looking at her. Making sure they don't touch.

Each flinch away makes her heart splinter.

But now's her chance to clear everything up. To tell him they can be together.

"Eric," she says softly, hating the way he winces. "There was a misunderstanding, but you left before I could tell you."

His gaze flickers to her, never has a chance to settle, before he looks away again. "There's nothing to discuss."

"No, there's everything to discuss." Ada takes a step closer, the truth aching to be said. "I'm not Tristan's soulmate. I picked up the wrong stone. I'm the Virgo."

This time, his gaze shoots back to hers and stays there. The gray depths are full of shock. Disbelief. And the love that's been her foundation her whole life. "What?" he whispers.

She nods, tears stinging her eyes. "It was my powers that lit up the Gemini stone, because I couldn't control them. But my suit wouldn't appear." She smiles tremulously. "And my stone was always with me, in my locket." She lifts it up to show him, even though he's seen it a thousand times before. "I figured out how to open it."

His gaze flickers to it, then finds hers again. "That's…great."

How many hours had they spent trying to get it open? When all it took was one word—akash.

Ada takes another tentative step forward, leaving only a few inches between them. "Do you realize what that means?"

They can be together.

She can control her powers.

Nothing can keep them apart now.

Something shifts, the briefest flash that crosses his handsome face, but Ada sees it. His features are more familiar to her than her own. A thread of uneasiness winds its way around her heart.

"Eric?"

His brows contract as the edges of his lips turn down. "We were never really together, Ada. It was always you, calling the shots, and me tagging along."

She can't speak. Because he's telling the truth. She took that for granted.

"And I was happy to do that, until you forgot to ask me if that was okay."

The raw agony twisting his face has Ada's throat clogging

with remorse and regret. Bitterness stains her tongue like acid.

"I'll come back with you. I'll be part of the Zodiacs because that's the right thing to do." He swallows. "But we're over."

She's frozen even though she's shattering. She's still even though everything is falling apart.

Eric takes a step back, creating a divide that never existed between them. "I'm sorry. I can't be hurt again. I just can't."

He turns and sits heavily in the nearest seat, dropping his head into his hands. They now have an entire flight to spend together.

Logan appears, his steps faltering as he sees them. Apart. Fractured. And hurting.

A single tear tracks down Ada's numb cheek.

It never occurred to her that she'd be too late.

TRISTAN

Tristan takes in the FBI agent he just crashed into, asking to have a word with him. Tall and thin and balding, he's frowning as if he's not here to have a social chat.

Which is fine by Tristan. He doesn't want to be having this conversation, either. "Sure, but hopefully it won't take too long or I'll miss my bus."

Agent Cadbury raises a brow. "I'd like to know what that group of homeless kids are doing outside the precinct."

Tristan shrugs. "No idea. Maybe they're protesting against the cost of burritos."

The agent hooks his thumbs in the belt of his slacks. "I just saw you leave them."

"Further proof I don't want anything to do with them," says Tristan, blank faced.

The man's frown deepens. "Do you know a young man named Malachi? I believe he's the ringleader."

"Nope."

"Are you sure? He's well known in these parts."

Tristan isn't going to mention he's just passing through. The less the FBI knows about him, the better.

"I have a good memory for names, I'm pretty sure I'd remember a Malachi."

Agent Cadbury's eyes narrow a fraction. "What's your name, son?"

For a brief second, Tristan considers giving a false one, but he quickly discounts it. If the man were to ask for ID, then lying is definitely going to get him on the radar. Besides, he won't be seeing Agent Jack Cadbury again.

"Tristan Ayers," he says. "I was just going home to my parents."

"And their names?"

Tristan's glad to see the agent isn't writing any of this down. "Zarius and Tess Ayers." He takes a step backward. "Now that we've ascertained I don't know anything, can I get going, please? My mom will worry if I'm not back soon."

The agent nods curtly. "Very well. Thank you for your time."

Tristan smiles. "Sure. See ya."

He goes to turn, but Agent Cadbury's voice stops him. "Mr. Ayers."

He turns around, keeping his smile in place even when he sees that the agent has a notebook out. "Yeah?"

"I just thought I'd let you know. A single run-in is rarely a cause for concern. But if I see your name again, then you'll have my attention."

Tristan salutes, keeping the motion jaunty even though his stomach is clenched. "Of course. Although I can't imagine why we'd run into each other again."

Not waiting for an answer, he turns and walks away. He heads straight for the bus stop, not stopping at the bakery, not caring if another petty crime happens right in front of him.

He's going back to the motel and then he, Zarius and Tess are leaving New York.

After this, they won't be back any time soon.

And Agent Jack Cadbury will forget he ever existed.

As Tristan and Jareth pull up at the address Ada gave them, Tristan realizes they're across the road from the motel they stayed at, all those years ago. He sits up a little straighter in the driver's seat, wondering if he's remembered wrong.

The place is closed down, and looks as if it's been like that for years. The gardens are overgrown, consisting exclusively of weeds. The walls have been graffitied and several windows are smashed. The sign saying *Moss View Motel* is covered in grime and…moss.

But it's definitely where they stayed.

"I know this place."

Jareth turns to him, surprised. "You do?"

"We stayed here. That time I was in New York."

Jareth glances at the rundown rows of rooms, the paint peeling off the blue doors. "That can't be a coincidence."

No, it really can't.

Tristan taps the screen on his phone in the way Ada showed him. It's time to learn if this technology is everything she's said it is. "Esther."

The reply is instant. "Yes, Tristan. How can I help?"

Tristan and Jareth glance at each other, impressed and a little unnerved.

"The address you sent us to," says Tristan. "Can you do a little bit of research on it? Past owners, last usage, that sort of thing?"

"Of course. I'll have a report shortly."

Silence fills the truck as Tristan stares through the windscreen. Has another Zodiac found this place, too?

He turns to Jareth. "Tell me more about Malachi."

"I'm not sure there's much to tell. He was an artist, like me. I think I related to him because he seemed different from so many of the other homeless kids. Like he hadn't grown up on the streets."

"But he never said that?"

Jareth shakes his head. "No. He just said he wanted to help. He was always connecting with kids, inviting them to the old apartment building, seeing if they needed anything."

"And that's how he got caught up in the gang violence?"

"I'm not sure. His death was kept on the low down."

Tristan nods, even though he's not sure what to make of it. It feels like there's a bunch of dots here that he's not connecting.

"Tristan?" Esther's voice comes straight through the car's speakers, making them both startle.

"You can access my car now?" he asks incredulously.

"Your car is connected to your phone via Bluetooth. Of course I can access it."

Jareth snorts out a laugh, and Tristan glares at him.

"Would you like me to call you?" Esther offers.

"No, this is fine." He sighs. Somehow, Esther is a clueless computer and considerate companion, all at once. The technology is amazing, it's just going to take a little getting used to. "What did you find out?"

"The Moss View Motel was purchased five years ago and stopped trading shortly after," she reports.

Tristan frowns. Right about the time he stayed here. "And do you know who bought it?"

"Yes."

He waits, then realizing that Esther took his question literally, he speaks again. "By whom?"

"Your parents, Tristan. Zarius and Tess Ayers were the owners of Moss View Motel."

Of all the answers he was expecting, that wasn't one of them. His parents bought the motel?

He shakes himself out of his shocked stupor. "Thanks, Esther."

"I'm here to help."

The truck goes silent again.

"But why?" Tristan wonders aloud. Why did his parents buy this place? It was dingy and run down even before it was left to die a slow death.

"Maybe it meant something special to them?" Jareth offers.

Tristan tries to remember if anything particular happened that day. He'd found Zarius and Tess pouring over the book, but they'd refused to let him see it so he'd stormed off. He'd assumed that running into Malachi and the near brush with Jareth, even Dyad, had been what had made the day exceptional.

But maybe he's missing something…

"We need to go in and have a look," he says. It's the only way they'll find out why this motel is significant. "We stayed in room number thirteen."

Tess always tried to stay in room thirteen, which was a challenge considering most places don't have a room thirteen due to superstition. If they found one, they always stayed in it. It was her way of honoring the number of Zodiacs they'd be uniting.

"Okay," says Jareth, his eyes scanning the numbers on the blue doors. Room thirteen is on the far end, one of the few doors where both brass numbers are still attached.

But before either of them can move, it opens. They both freeze, watching as a large man in a black shirt and jeans steps out. He glances one way, then the other, looking every part the bouncer outside a nightclub.

Tristan leans forward as he holds his breath. There shouldn't be anyone in there...

The door opens again then closes, even though no one's visible.

"Skins," breathes Jareth.

Chardis's goons are already in there.

Tristan's body coils. "I don't think Zarius and Tess bought the place to commemorate a belated Valentine's Day moment," he mutters.

"There must be something in there," says Jareth.

The book. Tristan never saw it again after they stayed here. He assumed they hid it somewhere so he wouldn't keep asking questions about it. It had worked—he'd returned his focus to training and searching for the other Zodiacs.

Zarius and Tess must've hidden it in the motel, then bought it to ensure no one stayed here ever again.

"Well, we need to make sure they don't get it," Tristan growls, opening his door as quietly as possible.

Jareth nods but doesn't move. "How many do you think are in there?"

"More than two," Tristan says with a shrug and a grin.

"I thought you'd say that," Jareth mutters. "And there's no one to call for backup."

"Nope. They're all dealing with their own dark matter disturbances. Turns out ours was Skins."

Jareth sighs. "Of course it was."

Tristan thumps his chest. "Lucky us, huh?"

He slips out of the car and Jareth follows. They won't have the element of surprise so there's only one way to approach this.

"We need to go on the offensive," he tells Jareth. "We'll get as close as we can, but then we have to be quick."

Jareth blanches but nods. "Can't wait."

Tucking his hands into his pockets, Tristan crosses the

road, Jareth beside him. Tristan can feel his heart rate already picking up in anticipation of the fight. Jareth's right, they have no idea how many Skins are inside the motel room. They're walking into a fight that could be far bigger and more brutal than they'd like.

But they don't have a choice. He knows deep in his bones that they don't want the book to fall in Chardis's evil hands.

They reach the pavement, and the Skin standing outside the room tenses as he glances in their direction.

"Get ready," Tristan says under his breath.

Jareth's nod is slight but enough to tell Tristan he heard him.

The Skin's head angles their way, his eyes covered by dark sunglasses. Although they can't see his eyes, it's clear they have his attention. His focus doesn't move from the two young men walking toward room number thirteen.

Tristan's muscles bunch and coil, ready to spring into action. "Now—"

Engines roar and tires squeal, making them both spin around, fists raised and ready to fight. Four black SUVs power into the parking lot, screeching to a halt outside the motel room.

Tristan watches in shock as men in dark suits pour out of the vehicles, guns drawn, and rush at the Skin.

"FBI! Put your hands up!"

The muscled man reaches behind him, no doubt to get his own firearm, but he's shot before he can reach it. The man falls to the ground and the agents—no doubt Nebula—swarm into the room.

Tristan instantly recognizes one of them—it's impossible to miss Jack's shiny globe for a head. Or the glare he throws Tristan's way before rushing into the room.

There are a handful of gunshots, several *thuds* and *crashes*, and it's all over.

"You're not going to leave yet, are you?" Jareth asks quietly.

Tristan shrugs. "I got the sense Jack wanted a word."

Jareth shakes his head. "And you're willing to hear what he has to say. As annoying as that is, I respect that."

Jack exits the room, eyes quickly moving to where Tristan and Jareth are, as if he's checking whether they ran. It's the exact reason Tristan decided to stay.

With Jack he has nothing to hide. Even as he has everything to hide.

"Tristan," Jack snaps as he approaches.

"Hey, Jack. Wassup?"

Just like Tristan knew it would, his greeting grates on Jack's nerves. "What are you doing here, Ayers?"

He shrugs. "Freakish coincidence. We were just out walking when you guys stormed this place like the fate of the world depends on it." He glances over Jack's shoulder. "Must be something interesting in there."

"There's never been a coincidence where you and I are concerned," Jack retorts, ignoring Tristan's observation. "Right back to the first time we met."

"We're fated mates," says Tristan, waggling his eyebrows.

A muscle twitches in Jack's jaw. "I'm nothing like you, Ayers. People meet you, and you either recruit them to your cause"—he sneers the word—"or they die."

He glares at Jareth and by the blaze in Jack's eyes, it's clear he's talking about his daughter. Tristan's gut tightens. And one day he'll learn that Logan is far more a part of this than he realizes.

"Anyway," says Tristan, meaning for the word to be said cheerily, only for it to be bitten out through his clenched teeth. "I hope you catch the bad guys."

When he finally figures out who they are.

"That's the plan," Jack snaps, spinning on his heel and

striding away, jerking his jacket closed as the lapel flaps open.

Tristan freezes as Jack strides away, blinking as he registers what he just saw tucked under Jack's arm.

"Tristan?" Jareth asks cautiously.

"Pitch," he mutters.

He was right. Zarius and Tess hid the book here.

And now Jack has it.

BRIELLE

"Welcome to D.C., and thank you for flying with Delta Airlines."

The seatbelt light overhead turns off as the pilot repeats the same thing first in German, then various other languages. At least, Brielle assumes it's the same thing even though the words sound so much more like a command than a pleasantry.

"Why do Germans always sound like they're yelling at you?" Cassandra grouses as she stares down at her phone.

Brielle smirks. This is why they're best friends. Even when they were arch enemies, they were always on the same wavelength.

The passengers at the front of the cabin begin rising to gather their luggage and disembark. Brielle resigns to wait, seeing as they're at the back.

"Any word from Logan?" Brielle asks.

Cassandra lets her shoulders sag and pouts as she looks up from the device in her hands. "No, nothing since he got on his plane."

"When were they due to land?"

Cassandra looks down at her phone again, then back up at Brielle. "Six o'clock Mexico time, but I have no idea what time that translates to here."

The pattern of rising heads finally reaches them, and Brielle and Cassandra grab their things and insert themselves into the aisle to follow the slowly trickling line off the plane.

"Well, maybe no news is good news," Brielle suggests from behind her.

Cassandra turns to hang her head in Brielle's direction. "When has that ever been the case in our line of work?"

Brielle purses her lips. Cassandra has a point.

"Nevermind about my man." Cassandra shakes her head, then tosses a coy look over her shoulder. "Let's talk about your new guy. He's a hottie. What's his name again? Kevin?"

The sudden change in topic has Brielle blushing for a moment. "Actually, it's Kerrim."

Cassandra scrunches up her face in a way that looks absolutely adorable. "What the hell kinda name is that?"

Brielle shrugs. "Honestly, I like it. It's different, like he is. He's not just another generic Steve or David."

"Or Kevin," Cassandra adds with a giggle.

Smirking, Brielle rolls her eyes and shakes her head. "Exactly."

They finally step onto the bridge and make their way down to the terminal.

"Well, whatever his name is, I'm just glad you're finally moving on from Tristan. That whole thing was just a big ol' dumpster fire."

The mention of his name has Brielle's heart tripping in her chest. She's definitely not over Tristan. Every time she sees him at HQ or school, her belly flutters. Every time their eyes meet, her soul sings in mournful longing. And apparently she can't even hear his name without suffering a minor cardiac episode.

No, she's not over him, but she's trying to be. She *needs* to be. And Kerrim is just the medicine to treat that disease.

Brielle clears her throat as they enter the gate lobby and head down the gangway. "Where are we supposed to go now?"

"The address is already programmed into your GPS, Brielle," comes the muffled voice of Esther from the front pocket of her jeans.

The response startles her—she's definitely not used to this female Jarvis that's infiltrated their lives and devices. One of many surprising new developments Ada's arrival brought with her.

She pulls her phone out of her pocket and sees that her screen is open to her maps app with the address plugged in.

"Great, so we get a cab," Cassandra says with a shrug, not seeming to mind the suped-up Alexa giving them directions.

"I have already arranged for one to pick you up at the departure parking lot," Esther informs. "The driver should be waiting in the main lobby holding a sign with your names on it."

Cassandra waggles her eyebrows at Brielle in happy surprise. "Esther, I think I love you."

Brielle holds back a frown.

"Thank you, Cassandra," Esther replies.

Brielle shoves her phone back into her pocket with a little more force than necessary. This whole AI thing feels a little too Terminator for her comfort level, but if Cassandra—and everyone else—is comfortable with it, she's going to go along with it.

She supposes it is nice that they didn't have to struggle with finding their way around this bustling city. She's never traveled anywhere outside of Mirror Point, save for the occasional trip to New York City, which she doesn't feel counts seeing as it's only a few miles away. Trying to navigate in a large city of such national importance wasn't something she was looking forward to. Now she doesn't have to worry about that, at least.

They find their way to the main lobby, and the driver holding the sign with their names isn't hard to spot. He's a short, chubby man with shaggy blond hair and a closely shaven beard framing a mouth that seems to be etched into a severe straight line.

The two approach him and Cassandra throws her Leo charm at him.

"You must be our driver," she greets him with a thousand-watt smile, batting her eyes in that flirtatious way of hers.

The straight line doesn't budge, but Brielle can swear there's a slight blush under all that facial hair. He gestures for them to follow him. Once outside, he ushers them to a yellow cab and opens the back door for them, and they slide in. When he gets into the driver's seat, Brielle leans forward and points to the address on her phone, and he nods and waves her away, assumedly already knowing their destination.

Judging by his absolute refusal to talk, Brielle guesses that he's a foreigner and probably speaks very little English. That makes sense for D.C. It's the international hub of the country and is sure to host a variety of foreign inhabitants.

The car whizzes them through the streets, and the heaven-reaching obelisk of the Washington Monument in the distance splits the setting sun in two. Brielle allows herself a moment to appreciate the power of this place. The beauty of the monuments and statues that litter the city. This place is living history, and she can't help but wonder what caused the spike in dark matter that sent them here. Is there another Zodiac waiting for them at their destination?

Her heart thuds like the strike of a gavel.

Could it be the true Gemini Princess?

She shudders and shakes the thought away. She's made her peace with the fact that the mystery girl will show up eventually, and she can't be broken-hearted by it when it happens. Not again. It's time to let Tristan go, to find her own happiness as he most certainly will.

The cab stops in front of a fancy-looking hotel, the tallest building on this street. It looks very international, with various countries' flags waving from its ledges. The driver thrusts the shifter into park, then climbs out and rounds the car to open their door.

"This is our destination?" Brielle asks him, hovering in her seat in front of the open door.

The driver grunts with a nod. She looks at her phone and sees that, yes, they are in the right place. She climbs out onto the curb, wondering who or what could be here that's so important to their cause. It must be another Zodiac.

But which one?

Cassandra follows after Brielle, carting her massive suitcase out behind her. "Thank you very much," she praises the driver.

Again, he doesn't reply, but walks back around the car sporting the same rosy cheeks.

"This is great," Cassandra says, trailing her suitcase up to the impressive front doors. "Now we don't have to look for a hotel! I can ditch this suitcase right away before we get started."

Brielle allows herself a giggle, figuring she might as well go with the flow, and follows Cassandra inside.

The interior is gorgeous, with intricate crown molding, columns lining the lobby, and again flags of all colors and stripes hanging on the walls. The marble floor is immaculate, like it's just one solid slab of uncut polished stone. Brielle can't help but feel very out of place here.

She follows Cassandra to the front desk.

"Do you have any rooms available?" Cassandra asks the clerk.

Brielle zones out as Cassandra turns her charm on the poor boy, no doubt securing them a room, and looks around for anything out of the ordinary.

"Excellent," she hears Cassandra say as she hoists her suitcase onto the counter. "Would you see to it that this is sent to our room? Thank you." Then she turns to Brielle. "So, where do we start?"

Brielle purses her lips in thought. "Let's take a look around."

"Great idea! I bet this place has a gift shop!" A flicker of excitement lights Cassandra's amber eyes.

"We're not here to shop," she scolds.

"I know." Cassandra rolls her eyes. "But we're here with the Zodiac credit card, and if we happen to find something we can't live without, then, you know, two birds."

Brielle bristles but decides not to chide Cassandra that the credit card is for emergencies only. She knows Cassandra is struggling to readjust from the loss of her own credit account since her parents disowned her. She hasn't exactly loved sharing a to-her-standards small living space with Brielle and Bea, so Brielle will give her some slack. But she draws the line at frivolous spending of money that belongs to Tristan.

"Come on." Brielle gestures for Cassandra to follow her as she heads toward a hallway, not sure what she's looking for. They wander past several empty lecture halls and conference rooms, all of which Brielle's sure her entire house could fit into.

Towards the end of this wing of the hall, they come across a conference room that's currently in use. Brielle almost walks past it completely, then stops to do a double take of the sign.

"Chardis Foundation Meeting."

Alarm bells go off in Brielle's head, and she freezes as she reads the sign over and over again.

"Cassandra, look." She points to the sign, and Cassandra narrows her eyes in a conspiratorial look.

Of one mind, they creep closer to the closed door and crack it open as silently as they can, peering inside. The room is a lecture hall filled with people, with a couple standing on stage speaking to the masses.

Cassandra turns to Brielle and nods her head toward the door before slipping inside. Brielle tries to hiss after her not to, but it's too late, and making any louder noises will alert the crowd of their presence. She has no choice but to follow Cassandra into the pits of hell.

She gently closes the door behind her and they hug the wall at the very back of the room. Brielle is beyond grateful that they haven't been noticed. All focus is on the people talking on stage.

"We've sent a contingent to collect the book, so it's only a matter of time before we can make our attack on the ark," says one of the speakers.

"Book?" Cassandra mouths the word to Brielle, her face most likely mirroring the questioning look on Brielle's face. What book could they be talking about? And what is the ark?

Brielle entertains for a moment that this could be a total coincidence. That this so-called Chardis Foundation has nothing to do with the Chardis they know, and that these people are all just ordinary humans gathered for an unrelated cause. She denies the obvious fact that something brought them here, and if it wasn't a Zodiac, then it could only mean one thing.

Skins.

But accepting that would mean accepting that they're trying to hide in a room full of their enemy, in such large numbers that they could never hope to escape if they're discovered.

Yep, feigning ignorance is a much more preferable option.

"Not only that, but the wormhole is large enough now to allow for a vessel of proper size to enter," says the other speaker.

And just like that, all of Brielle's hopes for another explanation are dashed.

"Which means that, very soon, we'll be able to go straight to the ark and eliminate the remaining enemy forces," the first speaker continues, and Brielle struggles to swallow around a sudden lump in her throat.

The Skins are after an arch. Enemy forces? Could they be talking about other Zodiacs? Outside of the Earth's solar system? Are they not all on Earth?

So many more questions flood Brielle's flustered mind, faster than she can give mental voice to them.

"Hey, you're late," hisses a voice nearby.

Both Brielle and Cassandra turn to the woman who's turned around to look at them, and too late, Brielle thinks about shielding her eyes when she sees the very clear ring of silver around the irises that stare at them.

"Hey!" the woman shouts, calling the attention of every head in the room to look at them. "What are you doing here? This is a private meeting."

White hot fear floods Brielle's nervous system, and she's momentarily frozen by it as she stares at the hundreds of eyes now on her and Cassandra.

"Oops, sorry, wrong room," Cassandra says with a nervous giggle, backing her and Brielle toward the door.

"Wait, that's Leo!" calls someone in the audience.

"And Libra!" calls another.

"Get them!" orders the second speaker.

Suddenly, all the heads in the theatre disappear, and Brielle instantly grabs Cassandra's hand and yanks her toward the door, sprinting out of the hall for dear life!

They run down the hall as fast as their feet can carry them, Cassandra taking the lead with her years of track experience. Brielle looks behind her as they run. She can't see anyone, but she can hear the echo of slapping feet and see the door propped open, meaning they're absolutely being followed.

What do they do? Where do they go? She'd like to think that Skins wouldn't attack them in such a public place, but she's sure Chardis could easily spin whatever altercation might happen as some tragic accident. They're not safe just because they're in the most publicized city in the country.

They need to find shelter. Now!

"Esther, we need an escape route now!" she yells, knowing her watch can hear her.

"Calculating," responds Esther immediately. Then a second later, "Turn right, now." Though the voice is calm and robotic, Brielle can hear the urgency in the command.

She does what the voice says without hesitation, and the turn leads them to a seeming dead end. Before she can ask what they're supposed to do, Esther instructs, "Push on the wall. There's a hidden service door. They won't find you if you act quickly."

Cassandra shoves at the wall, and sure enough, a seam in the wall parts and slides open, revealing a secret compartment. The two hastily slip inside just before the hidden door slides shut once more. Holding their breath, Brielle and Cassandra press themselves against the back wall of the chamber, pretending they're part of the bricks, listening to the parade of slapping feet on the marble that passes them.

After a moment, Cassandra takes in a breath to speak, but Brielle slaps her hand over her mouth to stop her. They're not out of the woods yet. They need to be absolutely certain the Skins are gone.

They remain like that for long moments, with Brielle's hand firmly clasped over Cassandra's mouth, listening intently to everything on the other side of the drywall. Until Cassandra's breathing regulates and she slaps Brielle's hand away.

"I could've incinerated all of them," she complain-whispers.

Brielle resists the urge to tell her all the ways in which that would have been a poor move on their part. They don't need more press, good or bad. And something like that would have definitely been bad press.

With utmost hesitation, Brielle creeps along the hidden corridor, beckoning Cassandra to follow her.

"If you continue down this hallway, it will take you to the kitchens," states Esther's voice in a much softer tone than before. She knows they're trying to be quiet? "From there, you can take the service exit. Your chance of being discovered there is approximately two percent."

"I'll take those odds," hisses Cassandra. "Thanks, Esther."

"You're welcome, Cassandra." The voice comes from Cassandra's phone this time.

They continue down the hall just as Esther had instructed, and sure enough, the corridor leads to the kitchens. The staff don't seem to notice or care that they're here, so they tiptoe through the aisles until they reach the exit into the staff parking lot.

After a moment with no sign of Skins, Brielle pulls out her phone. "Esther, call Tristan. We have a huge problem!"

13

ERIC

E ric stumbles over the threshold of the front door as he enters their not-so-abandoned apartment. He's still pissed at Ada, and the whole thing has his attention diverted away from his feet, apparently.

She insisted that she wasn't fooling around with that dude Carlton, but that she was only working for him. Whatever the truth of it, she'd still kept that from Eric. How could they truly be a couple if she's not willing to be honest with him?

"Hey, just the two people I wanted to see!" Malachi calls from his computer as they come inside. He beckons them with an excited wave.

Eric doesn't really want to chat right now, but he owes it to Malachi to hear whatever he has to share with them. They would be out on the streets if it weren't for him.

Once they're seated at the torn couch on either side of Malachi, Eric sees that his screen is open to Google Voice— few of the kids living here have phones, but they all have laptops and have found this particular website to be very handy for communication.

"I met this guy earlier today, he helped us with Jareth," Malachi says. "When I told him you two were a couple of UFO fanatics, he said he was also interested in aliens and wanted to talk with you."

Eric sighs. While he's more than a UFO fanatic, he doesn't feel like wasting his time talking to some random kid off the street about the possibilities of extraterrestrials, especially if the kid wasn't interested enough to stick around.

"Okay, well, why is he calling instead of coming here in person?"

"He was only passing through with his parents," Malachi explains. "But I told him you two knew everything there was to know about alien trivia and history and figured it was the least I could do to connect the two of you for his help."

Eric hangs his head. Malachi is a bleeding heart, always doing what he can to help others.

"Sure, we can answer some questions," Ada says, leaning toward the laptop.

"Great, let me call him." Malachi enters in a phone number and hits the call button.

After three rings, a young male voice answers, "Hello?"

"Hey Tristan, it's Malachi. My alien expert friends are back and willing to talk."

"Hi there," Ada says, waving at the screen even though the guy on the other line can't hear her.

"Hi," Eric says with half her enthusiasm.

"Thanks for calling, I appreciate it," the guy says. "How did you two get into aliens?"

Ada and Eric exchange a glance. He doesn't have an answer for that.

"Everyone has their hobbies," Ada replies dismissively.

"Fair enough," the guy chuckles. "How do you come across your information? Where do you do your research? Have you seen anything yourselves?"

"We haven't been abducted or probed, if that's what you mean," Eric says, the corners of his lips curling at the ridiculousness of that whole stereotype. He doesn't know where it came from, but real aliens don't do that sort of thing. Honestly, when humans find a new species, they don't stick something up that creature's bum to dig for information, then return them to where they found them. If anything, humans would dissect the creature, and then there's nothing left to set free.

Why should far more intelligent alien life be any different?

A snort sounds from the laptop's speakers. "Good, you may actually be a reliable source of information then."

They all share a laugh. Maybe this guy isn't so bad after all.

"As far as how we get our intel," Ada begins, braiding her fingers in front of her as she braces her elbows on her knees. "Let's just say we know our way around computers. We know how to find what people don't want us to find. And we've done enough research to suss out the facts from the baloney."

"Like abductions and probing," Eric adds with a chuckle.

Ada giggles, the sweet sound softening his heart toward her. This is why he never can stay mad at her—because he loves absolutely every single thing about her. From the sound of her breathing to the way she chews on her bottom lip when she's thinking about something. From her huge mass of fiery curls to the way she hypes up before a sneeze only to make the smallest and cutest squeak.

"I had assumed you were good with computers, seeing as you're calling me from one," the guy says.

Eric arches a brow and glances at Ada, whose nose is wrinkling in surprise. "How did you know that?"

"It's the way the sound comes through," the guy explains.

"Not as crisp as if you're talking right into a phone mic, but not as distant as if you were talking to me on speaker phone."

Malachi puts the back of his hand in front of his mouth to whisper, "Wow, this kid's a smart cookie."

Eric nods, impressed. "What do you want to know?" They're not dealing with just some run-of-the-mill UFO fanatic who geeks out at AlienCon. No, this kid is something different. Someone like them. Eric is disappointed now that they hadn't gotten to meet face to face.

The guy lets out a breath. "I'm looking for any information you might have on crashed pods."

"Pods?" Ada askes, craning her neck forward as if she thought she misheard him. "What sort of pods?"

"Small, one-person spaceships, essentially," he clarifies.

Eric and Ada think about that for a moment. Eric has never heard of any sightings of such a thing. But it's exactly that that has him interested. "I'm not sure we've heard anything about such vessels. Can you give us any other information that might help?"

"Well..." He drags on that one syllable, as if debating whether or not to continue. "Around twelve years ago, there would have been several crashes around the United States, and possibly Canada and Mexico."

"Twelve years ago, you say?" Ada asks, the tone in her voice alerting Eric that she's thought of something.

"Yes."

She wags her finger at the laptop. "Come to think of it, there were reports of sightings of meteorites streaking the sky on a night that there was no meteor shower on any country's radar. That was about twelve years ago."

"Really?" The guy's voice is pitched higher in excitement. "Where were the sightings?"

Ada shakes her head slowly once, opening her hands in a gesture of uncertainty. "Er, I don't recall at the moment. It was such a seemingly insignificant story that I didn't commit the details to memory. But if you want, I can round up the different reports and get them to you somehow."

"That would be great!" the kid exclaims. "I'll give you my email address—"

"No!" Ada cuts him off. "We don't freely exchange any form of direct contact with anyone we don't know and trust. You must understand."

"Hmm, okay... Well, seeing as you're so handy with computers, have you ever thought about starting a sort of internet forum for like-minded people like us? You could post those reports, and any other resources you come across on there, and maybe others will join and do the same."

Eric frowns thoughtfully. "That's not a bad idea, actually."

"You could call it UFOFanatics," the guy teases with a laugh.

Ada claps her hands. "I like it! I'll start it up this afternoon, in fact! And I'll post the reports tonight."

"Awesome! Can't wait to be your first member!"

"Thanks for the great idea," Eric says. "What's your name again?"

"Tristan," the guy says. "What's yours?"

Eric and Ada exchange another glance. Then a twinkle comes to Ada's eyes and she says, "You can call me Dyad."

Eric isn't sure why that memory invades his twilight consciousness as he fights sleep on the plane. But once it enters his mind, he can't let it go.

That was *the* Tristan that they spoke to all those years ago. They'd never heard from him again since that afternoon, but Eric had assumed that their first member GeminiI had been him. That website had been a great source of passive income for them once advertisers started buying ad placements and videos they uploaded had gone viral.

It's amazing to realize that their success with it had all started with Tristan. They'd met him—so to speak—five years ago, and he'd had no idea they were two of the Zodiacs he was searching for. And he and Ada had no idea that Tristan had the answers to the questions they'd spent their lives pondering.

What if the Zodiacs are meant to always find each other? They'd met Jareth back then, as well, never knowing he was more than some punk kid. Tristan has found six of the Zodiacs already. And if he'd come across the two of them before, and Jareth, who knows who else he might have met throughout the years that will turn out to be one of them, or who Eric and Ada might have met.

It would've been nice to think that Malachi might've been one. He was the most helpful person Eric had ever known. But if he had been, it would mean they'd lost a Zodiac.

Eric and Ada had moved on from the shelter shortly after starting the website, using the money she'd made from working for that douche bag Carlton to fund their own small studio apartment. A few days later, they learned Malachi had died. Eric had always felt guilty, like if they hadn't left, maybe Malachi would still be alive. Eric and Ada could've protected him.

He knows that's a stupid thought. Malachi was killed in some alley all by himself, clearly doing something shady. They wouldn't have been with him, therefore they couldn't have done anything to stop it.

A *ding* sounds from the plane's speakers, followed by the sultry sound of the male pilot's voice. "Passengers, we're lowering into the New York City airspace and will be landing shortly. Please put your tray tables into the upright and locked positions as we make our descent."

Ada puts her hand over his as the plane starts to tilt downward and the pressure builds in Eric's ears, but he slips it out from under her grasp and looks out the window.

He's not ready to feel her touch right now. Because even though he still loves everything about her, he also still can't trust her.

14

ADA

Ada curls up on the couch, her laptop resting on her knees. Eric sits beside her, holding an open packet of crisps. "Almost done?" He pops one in his mouth, crunching down as he slips an arm around her shoulders.

Her eyes don't leave the screen as she reaches over and gets her own crisp. "Just about." She snuggles in a little closer. "This is one of my biggest ones yet."

She can already feel Eric frowning. "More stuff for Carlton?" He almost sneers the last word.

But Ada shakes her head. "This is my own hack."

The work for Carlton has been feeling less and less comfortable. Even as they sit in the most comfortable place they've ever had. Ada rests her head on Eric's shoulder, letting out a sigh. "This little apartment is pretty amazing."

It's small and basic, but this is the first time they've had somewhere of their own. Rented under a pseudonym, paid for with her income from Carlton.

Eric's arm tightens. "It really is. It's home."

She looks up at him, eyes roaming over his handsome features. "You're my home."

His breath catches as his eyes flare. "And you're mine."

Joy soars through Ada. They've always been inseparable. The best of friends. But that changed recently. She's become aware of the breadth of Eric's shoulders. Of the heat of his skin. Of the lushness of his lips…

Friends is no longer enough.

Her laptop dings, startling her out of the growing awareness heating her blood. She looks back at the screen, then whoops with victory. "Mission accomplished!"

Eric peers closer. "Wow. That's a lot of money."

"Rent is sorted," she announces with a flourish. "At least for a couple of months."

"Who did we swindle this time?" Eric says jokingly, but she can see the slight strain around his eyes.

"No one," she beams. "Dyad may or may not have hacked into a large corporation. Then showed them the data he or she downloaded and sold it back, along with the information on their digital security weaknesses."

Eric's brows hike up. "Nice."

She shrugs. "I don't want to steal. And now we'll have some money left over for kids back at the apartment block."

Eric's smile is almost blinding. "That's a great idea. We can get them food and clothes."

"Exactly. Now that Malachi's gone, they need someone to look after them."

"You're amazing, Ada."

The huskiness in his tone has her pausing. The warm, rough edge rasps over her skin, making it heat.

"I wouldn't do any of this without you, Eric."

Without him, there's no reason to do anything. Eric is her reason for breathing.

His gaze drops to her lips, making them part on a silent intake of breath. Does he feel it, too?

"Ada," he whispers, the one word sending shivers down her spine.

She wants to say his name back with just as much longing, but her throat is clogged with emotion. Instead, she shows him.

She pushes the laptop away, barely noticing where it lands, as she leans into him. Then presses her mouth to his.

And finds heaven. Nirvana. Home.

Eric groans, spearing his fingers into her hair and trapping her where she is, increasing the pressure on her mouth.

Yes! her soul cries. *More!* her heart demands.

Ada climbs closer, heat spiking along her nerves. It makes her restless. Edgy. Hungry. Her hands come up to cup his face, desire skipping along her skin. She wants to touch Eric everywhere.

"Ouch," he hisses, pulling back with a jerk.

She yanks her hands back, knowing exactly what's happened. She curls her fingers in so tight, the nails bite into her palms. No, not with Eric…

He rubs his cheek ruefully. "Our chemistry is certainly explosive," he jokes.

Ada suppresses a frown. Does this mean she can't touch Eric the way she wants to?

He leans forward. "Hey, maybe we just have to take it a little slower."

"Maybe." Except she's never been able to control her powers. And there's no one she feels more strongly about than Eric. "I don't want to hurt you."

He slips a finger under her chin, raising her gaze to his. "I love you, Ada. Nothing could keep me away."

Her breath disintegrates. She suspected. She hoped. But they've never said the words.

"I love you, too, Eric. With everything I have."

His eyes fill with such tenderness and joy that Ada is

climbing on his lap before she's even realized it. Her hands brush his chest, right over his heart, and he jolts.

She instantly retreats. "Sorry."

"Never apologize," he says earnestly. He shrugs, grinning. "It got the old ticker going, that's for sure!"

Except, how do they move beyond friendship if she's going to zap him each time they get hot and heavy?

A knock on the door has them both stilling. They haven't told anyone they're here. Eric frowns. "Did you order pizza?"

"Nope. I was thinking we'd get Mexican for dinner." It's Eric's favorite.

They both approach the door and Ada cautiously looks through the peephole. "Carlton?" she asks, surprised.

"Of course it is," Eric mutters.

Ada opens the door, unsure of how she feels that he's here. "Hey," she says. "How did you find me?"

Carlton raises a brow. "I'm fine, thank you for asking. And you used the same alias to rent this place as you did on some of the office accounts."

Dammit.

She feels Eric move a little closer. "Ah, what are you doing here, Carlton?"

"You didn't complete the last task I set for you yesterday."

Actually, once she saw it involved drug money, she didn't even start it. "Yeah, about that…" Now that she knows she can earn her own income, and far more ethically, two words are waiting to be said. "I quit."

Eric's hand falls on her shoulder, a silent show of support. And probably encouragement.

"I see," Carlton says, his eyes narrowed. "I'm sorry to hear that."

"Thank you for the opportunity," Ada hastily adds. "I really appreciate it. It's just that I'm ready to move onto other things."

"You figured you'd learned everything you needed to, huh?"

Ada stiffens. "I've certainly learned a lot, for which I'll always be grateful."

"You might want to think this through—"

"Ada's made her decision," Eric says, his voice as hard as steel. "Your line of work is…well, let's just say she doesn't want to get into trouble."

Surprisingly, Carlton smiles. "I understand." He turns away. "Let's just hope it's not too late."

Before Ada or Eric can ask what he means, Carlton strides away, his back stiff.

Ada shuts the door, feeling bad after Carlton helped her when she needed money, but glad she's out.

"You quit?" Eric asks, smiling widely.

"I know you weren't comfortable with it. And neither was I." She shrugs. "The job was a means to an end."

He takes her hands and squeezes them. "We have somewhere to live. Money. A cool Mexican place down the street. And each other."

"Jackpot," Ada murmurs, the happiness she sees in Eric's eyes echoing in her heart.

He pulls her back to the couch. "So, Dyad's a bit of a modern-day Robin Hood, huh?"

Ada blinks. "I hadn't thought of it that way."

"You always did want to help others," he says fondly. "Now, why don't we look at the menu for the Mexican place and go get an early dinner?"

Before she can answer, three loud thumps on the door have them both startling. She frowns. Has Carlton come back? Because he sure didn't seem happy…

"FBI! Open the door!"

Ada's blood ices in her veins.

Dyad's been found.

Ada wipes her hands down her face, resting her elbows on her desk in HQ. Of course that's the memory rising in her mind.

Her and Eric's first kiss.

Their happiness at having their own place.

And how her choices destroyed it. Just like she did with their relationship.

Quiet thuds down the stairs have her straightening. She knows Eric's footsteps. Just like she knows he'll pause in the doorway, then hesitate when he realizes they're the only two down here.

Is this how it's going to be? Awkward. Painful. Uncertain.

"Hello, Eric," says a voice through the speakers. "It's nice to have you here."

Ada spins around to see his eyebrows shoot up. "Ah, hey."

"That's Esther," Ada explains. "Our AI computer."

"You brought Esther to life?" Despite everything, Eric sounds impressed.

"I did." *Because I was so driven to find you...*

"Wow." He looks around. "Hi, Esther. Nice to finally meet you."

"Likewise, Eric. Now that you've been located I can redirect the significant part of my processing energy that had been assigned to find you."

Eric's gaze shoots to Ada. "Oh."

"Yes. Ada insisted those algorithms take priority."

Ada flushes but doesn't break eye contact. Eric needs to know how important it was to find him.

He looks away. "Well, it's good that it can be used for something else now," he mutters.

"I agree," says Esther. "Because I've just confirmed that the wormhole is changing and broadening."

Ada spins back. "It's what?"

"After Tristan insisted on upgrading my programming, I'm assuming that's a rhetorical question."

More clattering footsteps sound as Tristan and Jareth appear. Tristan grins when he sees Eric. "Good to have you back," he says, clapping him on the shoulder.

Eric nods. "Thanks."

Before Jareth can speak, Brielle and Cassandra enter HQ. "Boy, do we have a story to tell you!" announces Cassandra.

"What story?" asks Logan, arriving right behind them with Veronica.

Cassandra folds into his arms while Veronica gravitates toward Jareth. Ada sees that Eric notices it, too. Others are couples within their ranks.

Does any part of him wish they could be, too?

Looking away, she settles her gaze on Tristan. "I think my story might trump the others."

He stills. "Oh?"

"The wormhole is on the move again. It's getting bigger."

A hush falls over the room as each of the Zodiacs digests this. Jareth and Veronica move closer together. Logan and Cassandra glance at each other, their fingers weaving tightly.

And yet, Ada's never felt further away from Eric.

"Oh crap," Tristan groans, his voice sounding strangely far away. "Now I get a vision?"

15

TRISTAN

The darkness comes quickly, as if the vision is in a hurry. Tristan finds himself floating in space, endless black surrounding him broken by glittering specks of light. Suns and stars, so tiny, and yet each is a world of its own.

Tristan doubts he'll ever stop being humbled by the fact he and the Zodiacs have been tasked with keeping every inch of this vastness safe.

He turns, wondering why he's here, and gasps. A vibrant blue planet is in the distance, two white rings surrounding it. It's big and beautiful and breathtaking. A part of him wants to go to it. To see if there's life on it.

But the image fades, little more than a snapshot of the beauty that exists out here in space.

Tristan holds his breath, conscious the second vision is coming. He even closes his eyes for a brief moment, bracing himself. Nothing bad happened in the first vision.

The second will be the destruction they're supposed to prevent.

He's still not ready for what he finds when he opens his eyes. The blue planet is gone. Destroyed.

Tristan's now floating among nothing but debris. Rocks ranging from the size of a jagged meteor to a listless fleck of dust. His eyes widen as he does a slow turn. "No," he breathes.

How could an entire planet be smashed to smithereens like that?

One answer punches through Tristan's mind.

Chardis.

At the next blink, the scene disappears, and he finds himself once more in HQ. The Zodiacs look at him, faces painted with various shades of apprehension. And unfortunately, it's warranted.

He's just seen a blue planet at the same point in time, but with two very different outcomes.

In one, it and every life on it survives.

In the other, it's totally obliterated.

16

BRIELLE

A few days have passed since the whole encounter with Ada and Carlton at the ice cream shop, and no sign of Carlton. Brielle tries to consider herself lucky, that she doesn't need more enviable objects in her life, and that maybe Ada and Carlton are better off together than Brielle might be with him as a friend.

But still, his lack of contact stings a little bit. She'd thought he was her first true friend since Cassandra's absence, and the reassurance that such a thing isn't the case only makes her feel more alone.

At school, Cassandra seems to be thriving. She's no longer even making eye contact with Brielle—she's acting like Brielle doesn't exist. More salt in the wound. And she's making fast friends with the cheerleaders and track team students.

Brielle has tried to be happy for her. At least one of them made it out of the stigma of being parentless. But up until that fateful day that Cassandra left, she'd been Brielle's only friend. Her best friend.

So now she's down a Cassandra, and down a Carlton.

How many more potential friends are you going to chase off, Brielle? she asks herself as she trims the hedges in the orphanage garden.

"Hey stranger," says a painfully familiar voice.

Brielle looks up, about to angrily decapitate a wayward branch, to see Carlton on the other side of the hedge.

Refocusing on her task at hand, she says, "Hey," and continues to snip the branches that are most like her—the ones that don't fit in. Honestly, she can think of no more suitable punishment for listening to visions she shouldn't have than basically pruning natural manifestations of herself.

"I know things have gotten...weird between us the last week," he says, kicking at the ground with his hands in his pockets. "But...I wanted to make sure I said goodbye before I left."

"Left?" Her head pops up, and she freezes before snipping another twig. "You're leaving?"

He nods, face downcast, eyes glued to his shoes. "My father is uprooting the business, so I have to follow."

After a painful pause, and an almost equally painful swallow, Brielle continues her decapitation. "How does Ada feel about that?"

She doesn't look up, but she can see his face turn into a question mark in her peripheral vision. "Ada? What?"

"You two were flirting at the ice cream shack," Brielle states bluntly.

He laughs, making her feel more stupid than she already did. "We so were not flirting," he says, slapping his knee. "She's just doing some computer work for my father."

Brielle's face scrunches in confusion. If that's so, then why did Ada feel guilty for being around Carlton?

Not that it matters now.

"Is that why you've been avoiding me?" He inclines his head toward her, a brow raised surreptitiously.

She shrugs, continuing her work. Regardless of the reason for their distance, it no longer matters. He's leaving, and she feels stupid for pushing him away while she could've been enjoying his friendship. But she's too proud to admit that right now.

"Anyway, I'm expected back," he says after clearing his throat through an awkward silence. "I just didn't want to leave without saying goodbye. I hope I'll see you again."

Too late, she lifts her head from her chore to say all the things she'd been wanting to say, only to see him several feet away, his back toward her as he heads toward his next destination. One that doesn't have her in it.

Great, Brielle. You've managed to chase away the only two people who gave a crap about you, and now you're alone again.

After standing and staring after him for a few long minutes, as his back disappears around a corner, she grits her teeth and continues the task she was given.

She just has to face facts—she's meant to be alone.

"Where's Kerrim?" Brielle asks.

The space behind the counter where Kerrim usually sexily leans is empty.

Madge shrugs, pausing her lazy wiping of the sneeze guard on the other side. "Don't know. He called a few days ago and said he had emergency family matters and wouldn't be in for a while." She frowns, then sighs, continuing moving the rag in circles over the thick plastic. "I may have to find another server to replace him if he doesn't at least call in soon."

Brielle's shoulders slump as she ties the Creamy Dreams apron around her waist.

Since getting back from that nightmare trip to D.C.,

Brielle hadn't heard from Kerrim at all. She'd begun to wonder if he was purposely avoiding her texts and calls. But now that she knows Madge hasn't heard from him either, she's concerned for him.

Did he lose a loved one and had to go somewhere out of cell range for their funeral? Was he inconsolably sad and didn't want to talk to anyone, not even her?

Or had something more sinister happened? Had Chardis somehow discovered that Kerrim's important to one of the Zodiacs and abducted him, or worse?

A bolt of panic strikes through her, and she has to shake her head to release herself from that terrible thought.

A throat clears to her left, making her startle back to the present to see a customer waiting at the counter. She plasters on a smile. "How can I help you?"

The afternoon offers a steady flow of customers, not to the point that the volume is stressful, but just enough to keep Brielle from dwelling in the dark corners of her thoughts. It also helps the time pass more quickly, for which she's both grateful and reluctant.

When she gets off work, she and Bea are supposed to visit Frank at the New York City Detention Center. Of course, Brielle is eager to see him. She misses him so much. He really has become the father she never had and always dreamed of, and her life seems so empty now without him. But as much as she wants to see him, she's dreading exactly what she will see. What if he's been getting beaten up in there and his face is all bruised? She knows she'll fall apart if he's anything less than his normal self, and there won't be damn thing she can do about it.

"Are you ready to go?" sounds Bea's voice from the door at the end of Brielle's shift.

Unable to voice any of her conflicting feelings at the question, she simply nods, then hangs up her apron on a free hook on the back wall before rounding the counter to follow Bea out.

"Did you let Cassandra know we'll be home late?" Bea asks as they get into the car.

Brielle pulls the belt across her torso and buckles in, humming in affirmation.

Bea shakes her head, her eyes puffy as she gruffly jerks the shifter into drive. "I can't believe that awful man would throw his own daughter out onto the street. Poor girl."

Brielle bites her tongue. Bea doesn't know the half of the cruelty Cassandra's father has put her through, physically abusing her every time she so much as sneezed in his direction since he adopted her.

"You were so right to warn Frank against making that deal with him," Bea continues through gritted teeth, driving a little too quickly down the road. "I just wish we'd listened to you then." She turns rueful mahogany eyes on Brielle, her brow pinching in the middle. "I'm so sorry."

Brielle shakes her head. "It's okay, don't go beating yourself up for it. This is no one's fault except for Richard Sinclair."

Bea nods, her face returning to its angry, vengeful mask as she returns it toward the road. "I don't know how he got away with it. I've had the finest crypto-accountants looking through every single transaction, and they can't find anything to implicate Mr. Sinclair."

A low sound rumbles deep in Bea's throat, a cross between a wolf's growl and jungle cat's warning purr. It would be a frightening sound if it weren't aimed at the very man Brielle wishes would get eaten by both animals. At the same time.

"But don't worry, we'll find something eventually," Bea adds after a cleansing exhale. "We still have time before the trial."

"Do we know when it's set for yet?" Brielle asks, dread and hope playing tug-of-war with her tone.

Bea shakes her head as they turn toward the entrance of the barbed-wire-fenced enclosure. "No. I just hope Frank can last in there until whenever they decide to set it. It could be months."

"Or it could be next week," Brielle adds, which wouldn't be great either as they have no evidence of his innocence.

"We'll just keep hoping for a miracle," Bea sighs before rolling down her window for the guard at the entrance booth.

They get signed in, park, and get out of the car. Bea's movements are just as hesitant as Brielle's, and Brielle realizes her mom is as conflicted about coming here as she is.

Only probably worse. Frank isn't someone she's only known and grown to care for over the past few months. No, to Bea, Frank is her true love, the man she's been married to for years. Whatever trepidations Brielle might feel, she's sure Bea's feeling them tenfold.

Shoving her own fears aside and mustering a supportive smile, she takes Bea's hand and gives it an encouraging squeeze.

"Everything will work out, Bea. I promise."

Bea's shoulders lower every so slightly, the tension in her neck and arms visibly receding. "You're right." She fusses with her hair for a moment. "Let's go see our guy."

17

ERIC

"Can I get a name for your hotel room?"

The receptionist is only a few years older than them, and her face is sweetly pretty and innocent as she asks for a name.

"Smith," he and Ada reply in chorus. Then they look at each other, surprised at their synchronism, and share a smile.

When he turns back to the receptionist, a confused, quizzical expression wrinkles her forehead.

"Enrique Smith," Eric offers.

The girl pauses, staring at them blankly for a minute, then refocuses on her computer screen. "Oooo-kay. Can I have a credit card for incidentals?"

Ada slaps her hand down on the desk, sliding a wad of cash toward the girl. "That won't be necessary." Ada leans forward and winks at her. "And there's a Benjamin in it for you if you make this go smoothly."

A blush creeping into her cheeks, the receptionist covers the cash with her hand and slides it the rest of the way over the desk until it disappears over the edge. She taps away for a moment, then places a key on the desk in front of them.

"Mr. and Mrs. Smith, you'll be in room 208. Thank you, and enjoy your stay with us."

When they don't immediately take the key, she gives them a curt nod toward the elevator, as if to hurry them along.

Ada needs no further invitation and snatches the key, then tugs Eric toward the elevator. It's not until the doors slide closed and Ada presses the second floor button that Eric's pulse slows to near normal rhythm.

They narrowly escaped the FBI banging on their door by scurrying down the back staircase out their window. So much for having a place of their own.

It didn't take long for them to figure out that Carlton had outed them. There was no other way they could've detected Ada's encrypted IP address, let alone link it back directly to their new apartment.

Rat bastard! Eric knew from the instant he eyed that slimeball that he was bad news.

At least they're safe now, for the time being. But for how long? Ada's wanted by the freaking FBI! Those A-holes don't give up once they've spotted you—like a bloodhound once it's got your scent, you're toast.

When the doors open, Ada carries the only possession worth a damn to either of them—her laptop Esther—toward their room. They silently tread down the hall, as if expecting to wake a slumbering FBI agent behind one of the doors they pass, and turn the key into the lock. Opening the door, they slip hastily inside and close and lock it behind them.

Ada lets out a heavy breath through pursed, beautiful lips as she presses against the closed door.

He lets out a sigh of relief as well. They're safe. For now.

After a few seconds with no stomping feet in the hallway, Ada kicks away from the door and gently, lovingly, sets the laptop on the bedside table. Then her eyes rest on the bed, staring at it for the longest time, before she quirks her eyes up at him with a playful glint in those lime-green irises.

"Shall we christen the new bed?"

Her words, paired with the waggle in her perfect auburn eyebrows, has his center both melting and raging at the same time. "D-didn't we try that already?" He can't help the stammer in his voice. He's nervous. And not just from the fact they barely escaped the FBI.

She sits on the bed, and his heart can't help but hiccup at the fact that she's trying to be provocative. It's extremely cute and endearing. And, admittedly, successful. She pats it. "You know what they say: 'Try, try, try again?'"

Is he actually blushing? He's not supposed to be the sensitive one in this scenario. But…with Ada…how can he not be?

She's his everything. And he wants her every bit as much as he loves and cares for her. And after his surprising bout of jealousy over Carlton, he recognizes that he needs to claim her before someone else more charming and seductive does.

He eagerly closes the distance and climbs onto the bed, gently but possessively taking her face into his free hand and pulling it to his lips.

Was it only less than an hour ago that they'd kissed for the first time? Her lips feel like…home. Like he's tasted them, felt them, a thousand times. And yet, he never wants to let his own part from hers. They fit so perfectly into each other. And when she opens her mouth to invite him in, their tongues caress, mouths opening and closing in the perfect rhythm.

Like they were made to kiss each other.

And so much more.

A pant sounds into his open mouth, and where her lips meet his, he feels a small but distinct *zap*.

Not again, he grouses internally.

Yet, he doesn't care. He doesn't want to stop, not even if it means a thousand zaps. Maybe he just needs to become immune to them. And that can only happen with practice.

Their kiss deepens as he ventures further into her delicious mouth, savoring the feel of her tongue against his as they dance and wrestle. Her tongue repeatedly shocks his in tiny bursts, the feeling like pop-rocks popping, only a bit more potent.

This isn't so bad, he tells himself. He's eaten pop-rocks dozens of times, even poured an entire bag in at once—*with* soda!—to see how much he could handle. He totally won that bet. This is just like that. Only, instead of winning a few measly trading cards, he's winning physical contact with the love of his life.

Their bodies move in-sync so that she lays on the bed and he hovers above her, barely pressing his weight on her as much as he dares.

Her fingertips find the bottom of his shirt and creep underneath, needing more skin-to-skin. The feel of her fingers on his bare back is heaven! So soft and acute and warm, sending tingles up his spine...

Until it's not just pleasurable tingles but actually shocks zinging him every time her skin comes in contact with his. Her sweet, gentle fingers trail an electric burn over his flesh as they reach up to his shoulder blades.

Just breathe through it, he tells himself. He *can* tolerate this. For her. For him. For *them.*

But within seconds of determining that claim in his mind, every succinct location that her body touches his sizzles with unbearable static prickles.

Until he can no longer bear it.

"Ah!" he screeches, jerking completely away from her like she's a high-voltage fence.

"What's wrong?" she says with the saddest pout on her delicate lips, panting heavily and looking up at him.

"I—you—it—ah!" He groans in frustration, jumping off the bed and raking his hands through his short blond tufts.

After seeing the look of instant rejection on his love's face, he immediately crumples to kneel at the side of the bed, taking her hand in his.

"It's the zaps," he admits, hating himself—and the circumstances—for it. "I thought I could grow immune to it. Let it hit me long enough until it didn't bother me anymore. But..."

"Oh no!" She jerks her hand away from his, glaring at as if it has wronged her. "I was hurting you!?" Her voice turns into a question at the end, and he hates hearing her fear and pain.

"Only a little," he lies, inching closer, but she only backs up against the headboard.

"I was hurting you," she repeats, this time with tears spilling down her lovely face.

His heart shreds down the middle, and he's surprised his blood isn't spilling down the bedsheets to puddle onto the floor. He instinctively, reflexively, closes in to scoop her into his arms.

No part of her is electric now, the static energy dulled by sorrow deeper than the deepest crevice in the ocean floor. "It's okay," he coos, soothingly patting down her frizzled orange ringlets. "We'll figure this out. We'll just have to go...*really* slow."

She hiccups a laugh. "I thought we already were. Does this mean we have to live like Amish people?"

His laugh is strangled by a tight throat. "I hope not. I'd hate to see you on a Rumspringa bender."

She throws her head back in a totally free, all-out laugh that lightens the dark mood in their hotel room.

They decide to just chastely cuddle and watch something on TV so they can both get some much needed shut-eye.

They can worry about electricity-cock-blocking powers and FBI agents tomorrow.

For now, it's just the two of them, being them, in blissful contentment.

Eric hates that he's thinking of their first failed attempt at intimacy, but as he's sitting so close to Ada, hovering over her shoulder as they both try to glean what information they can about the wormhole, he can't help it.

She smells so good, like sparky cinnamon and burnt sugar, all things hot and sweet.

"Eric, did you hear me?" she asks, looking at him over her shoulder.

"No, sorry, I was miles away for a second." He clears his throat and scoots back away from her an inch or two. "What were you saying?"

Her eyes narrow and she scoffs at him. "Come on, we need to stay focused! Some planet out there is in danger of being destroyed, and from Tristan's descriptions of it, it's not in our solar system. I don't think whatever force that gives Tristan these visions would let him see something he had no way of intervening in, so that means there must be a way to get to this far off planet, wherever it is." She turns back to the many screens in front of her. "Seeing as we measly humans haven't discovered light-speed yet, we have to assume that the wormhole works two ways."

Eric crosses his arms and chews his cheek as he ponders, trying not to notice how her green eyes light up when she's talking about a topic she's passionate about. "How do we figure that out? Are you suggesting we go to the wormhole in person and try it out?"

Ada's fiery curls bounce back and forth as she shakes her

head. "No, I'm definitely not willing to risk anyone's safety on such a gamble. We'll just have to use the science and facts at our disposal."

"Which are what, exactly?" Eric asks, boggled as to what she could be talking about.

"I've accessed the data stream of the NASA satellite that's observing the wormhole," comes Esther's voice from the speakers around the room, making him jump. Though he thinks it's cool as hell, it's definitely going to take some getting used to.

Swallowing down the pride he feels for Ada's AI accomplishment, he asks, "What are the variables they're monitoring?"

"Gravity fluctuations, radiation emissions, light spectrum variations, and the mass, volume and velocity of the particles escaping the event horizon," Esther responds.

Eric nods, trying to make sure he understands what each of those things really means. "Can you show us the data stream?"

One screen fills with a sophisticated black spreadsheet with numbers all in white. There's at least a dozen columns.

Eric hooks his fingers around his chin as he scans over the numbers.

"The problem is," Ada says after a moment of their silent examination, "I can't figure out how we're going to be able to tell if the wormhole is an entrance as well as an exit. I'm not exactly an expert in physics, so I'm not sure what to look for."

The fingers cupping his chin begin to rub along his jawline as he stares at the spreadsheet. He wouldn't claim to be a physicist, either, but he is a huge fan of documentaries, especially those about space. He looks at the numbers under the velocity column.

Of course, the asteroid had been going several hundred miles an hour, so he ignores that output. The other outputs don't seem to be close at all, or have anything to do with their size. In the case of black holes and whites, for instance, the theory at least is that matter goes into a black hole and shoots out of a white hole, making it a one way route. All matter that escapes through the white hole is going the same speed, and there's usually a lot of it.

Seeing as there's no huge stream of speeding particles, they're not dealing with a white hole. But then, he already knew that. The question is, can something enter the event horizon without getting obliterated, or can it pass through?

"Esther, can you show me just the data for the particles heading toward the wormhole?" he asks.

The spreadsheet changes to show all the negative integers under the velocity column bunched at the top.

"What are you thinking?" Ada asks, curiosity heightening the pitch of her voice.

Eric's eyes scan over the other columns of the top rows, focusing on the numbers under gravitons. It's just as he thought.

"The graviton values don't change the closer a particle gets to the event horizon," he exclaims, staring at Ada with wide eyes.

Her pretty face scrunches in confusion, clearly not understanding what he knows it means. "Okay, so…?"

"So, that means the particles aren't getting crushed under immense gravity when they cross the point of no return," he explains, losing control of the volume of his voice in his excitement. "It means that they're going somewhere!"

Her eyes widen, too, as a smile spreads across her face. "Eric, you're a genius!" Suddenly, her arms wrap around his neck, her cinnamon scented curls caressing his face.

He'd forgotten how wonderful it felt to be so close to her, to feel her pressed against him…

When his arms don't close around her, she quickly jerks

back, a question on her slightly pouting lips and in the gentle crease in her brow.

Finally, he shakes his head and rises from his chair, taking a few steps back. "I just can't right now. I'm sorry. I think we both need time apart from each other. Time to figure out who we are on our own." Even though, apparently, who he's been so far on his own is someone who drinks way too much and will try any substance despite the risks.

She sucks in her bottom lip for a moment, her eyes rolling up in a failed attempt to hide the moisture building there. Seeing that sheen of pain makes his heart hurt, and he still feels the urge to take it away from her by whatever means necessary.

But his pride keeps him locked in place, keeps his mouth shut.

At last, she nods. "Okay. Whatever you need. I'll be here when you're ready. I'll always be here."

Eric has never felt more lost than he does as he stands there under her gaze. So he ambles awkwardly backward until he has enough sense to turn around and exit into the hallway.

After everything they've been through, after all the years of only wanting to get closer to her, Eric can't believe he's actively trying to increase the distance between them. And you know what?

It still hurts like hell.

18

ADA

Ada watches Eric walk out, clutching the arms of her chair with everything she has. If she doesn't, she'll go after him. And probably shake him.

Then beg him.

The whole time, wanting nothing more than to kiss him.

They can't throw everything they had away. Not now. Not when she finally has control of her powers.

But Eric needs time. He needs to know he can trust her after she's let him down more than once. After she broke his heart.

So, with a sigh, Ada turns back to the computer. Eric's insight into the wormhole was valuable. Now they have to decide what to do with it.

And she has no idea what that is. They can't exactly fly on up there and check it out. Although it's physically possible with their suits, it's far too dangerous. Who knows where the planet is. Why Chardis is targeting it.

Whether they can save it...

At the sound of footsteps down the stairs, Ada spins

around, excited before she registers they're not Eric's. These are lighter, a little slower. And yet, somehow heavier.

Brielle appears, glancing around HQ. "Oh, I thought everyone else was here?"

Ada shrugs. "They're upstairs eating pizza. Seems visions make people hungry."

Brielle frowns. "Tristan had another vision?"

"He saw a blue planet. In the first, it's intact. In the second..." she grimaces, "not so much. Chardis is really stepping things up."

Sitting down on the nearest chair, Brielle blinks. "He really is."

An entire planet could be destroyed. And if that happens, it's only a matter of time that Earth will be next. Who knows where he'll stop...

Brielle draws in a deep breath, as if she's fortifying herself. When her gaze returns to Ada, it's calm and determined. "We've ensured the vision where lives are saved is the one that becomes reality every other time. We'll do that again."

Ada grins, appreciating the quiet spunk in this girl. "Exactly my thoughts."

Brielle flashes a brief smile, then seems to hesitate.

Wondering if the same memory is hovering in Brielle's mind, Ada leans forward. "Do you remember?"

Brielle nods, obviously knowing what she's referring to. "I do."

"Sorry I was a bit...rude."

"I shouldn't have said what I did," Brielle says, shaking her head. "I didn't even know you."

You shouldn't do this.

Brielle ducks her head. "I was jealous of what you had with Carlton."

Ada blinks, not liking that someone else thought there

was something going on between her and that slimeball. "We weren't a thing, if that's what you're thinking."

"But you felt guilty. I could sense it," says Brielle with a puzzled frown. "And it had to do with Eric."

Flushing, Ada also pulls her head into her shoulders. "It's because of the work I was doing for Carlton. I knew Eric wouldn't approve."

But she desperately wanted to find a way for them to survive on their own, so they could be together. Forever.

And all she did was undermine Eric's trust in her. And then she annihilated that shaky foundation in her desperate search for answers to their powers.

Her mouth twists. "And then he called the FBI on us." Meaning they'd be on the run for years until they met the Zodiacs.

Brielle nods sadly. "He used us both." She chews her lip. "I just don't know what he wanted with me."

"A pretty girl by his side?"

Brielle blushes, looking away. "I doubt it was that." She shrugs. "Anyway, it's kind of cool that we've met before."

Ada beams. "I like the spin you put on things. Always looking on the bright side."

Brielle smiles back. "Have you seen the movie, *Annie*? I think it's growing up in an orphanage."

"I always liked Annie," grins Ada. "I related to the red curls."

"We both had something in common with her."

They smile at each other, and Ada realizes they've just connected. Possibly become friends.

It feels good.

The clatter of footsteps has them both turning as Tristan bursts into the room, waving a slice of pizza. "I've got an idea —" He stops in his tracks when he sees Brielle, the pizza forgotten. "Oh, hey. How was your dad?"

She pulls up a half-smile. "Staying strong."

"That's good," he says quietly. "I know it had to be tough."

Brielle nods, her gaze sliding away. "Yeah, it was."

Ada sits very still in her chair, conscious of the tension hanging in the air, although she suspects it has little to do with Brielle's father being in jail. It's obvious these two have feelings for each other.

And yet Tristan has a Gemini soulmate out there, waiting for him.

Wow. Complicated, much?

Ada clears her throat. "You had an idea, Tristan?"

He jolts, throwing the pizza in a nearby trash can as if he's no longer hungry. "I can't just sit around, waiting to find out about that planet or where it is. So, I think we should look for the book."

There are more footsteps, and the rest of the team file into HQ, Eric up the rear. The Zodiacs fan out through the room, Veronica still munching on pizza, Cassandra shaking her head and muttering about empty calories. Jareth is carrying a mug of what smells like some sort of herbal tea.

"The book?" Eric asks, keeping his gaze fastened on Tristan.

It stings as Ada realizes Eric's eyes always found her the minute he entered a room. Any warm vibes that had kindled after the talk with Brielle are quickly doused.

"The one that Zarius and Tess hid, and Jack stole," Tristan explains. "It has information about the refuge."

"The refuge?" Eric repeats again.

"Some ship out in space, carrying all the refugees fleeing from Chardis," says Brielle. "Tristan's right. It's important we find it, more than ever."

Because a planet could be destroyed.

"You want to talk to my father?" Veronica asks, her eyebrows raised. She and Logan glance at each other.

Tristan grins. "I love a good chat with Jack. In fact, I was hoping you'd line it up for me."

Veronica shrugs. "I suppose it's worth a try." Pulling out her phone, she goes back up the stairs, taking another bite of her pizza.

"No wonder Chardis wanted the book," Ada muses.

"And I doubt we want that information in Nebula's hands, either," adds Eric, his gaze finally reaching her.

"Good point. Jack thinks all aliens are the enemy."

Logan shifts a little, looking uncomfortable. "One day he'll learn the truth."

Cassandra wraps herself around his arm. "Even if he doesn't, he'll always love you, no matter what." Her eyes twinkle. "I mean, how could he not? You're smart, brave and hot."

Logan chuckles. "I'm not sure that's how he'd describe me."

Cassandra smiles, not bothering to argue. Ada suspects her goal was to see a smile back on Logan's face.

Veronica appears, looking a little shocked. "Dad said he's willing to meet." She wrinkles her nose. "In an hour."

Tristan nods. "Text him it's a date." He scans the Zodiacs in the room. "Ada and Eric, you stay here and keep an eye on the wormhole."

Ada's heart jolts at the chance to spend more time with Eric. Even Tristan's noticed how well they work together.

"Veronica and Logan, you two can't be anywhere near this," Tristan continues. "And Jareth and Cassandra can't by extension."

Cassandra huffs but doesn't object. She and Jareth are dating Logan and Veronica. And the Zodiacs can't afford to get Jack offside as they negotiate for the book.

Tristan's gaze zeroes in on Brielle. "Which leaves the two

of us." His mouth twists into a wry smile. "He'll probably listen to you more, anyway."

Jareth chuckles. "She's the one who talked most of us into being here. If anyone can do it, Brielle can."

A delicate pink blooms across her cheeks. "I'll bring brownies," she jokes. Turning serious again, she looks back at Tristan. "Let's go get the book."

The smile that climbs up his face has Ada blinking. Eric used to smile at her like that.

She watches along with the other Zodiacs as they leave, realizing two things.

Everyone loves Brielle.

Including Tristan.

Actually, make that three things.

There are some obstacles that love can't conquer.

19

BRIELLE

Even though it's only been a few days since he said goodbye, Carlton's absence has only darkened the metaphorical rain clouds above Brielle's head that never seem to go away.

This afternoon, as she walks back to the orphanage from school, those rain clouds are a very physical thing, threatening to let loose their liquid bounty on her at any minute. But not even that is enough to make her go any faster than a sluggish walk along the sidewalk. She just doesn't have the energy to scurry home, or to care whether she gets soaked before reaching there.

As she rounds a corner behind the gas station, the sound of quickly approaching feet slapping the pavement ahead has her looking up from her own feet. But not soon enough.

Whack!

The impact of a medium-sized body slamming into her shoulder sends her falling to the ground, landing painfully on her butt, her palms scraping on the sidewalk as she fails to catch herself.

"Sorry," she hisses through the various aches, looking

over her shoulder and preparing to offer help to whoever she'd crashed into.

The boy, a couple years older than her, is already pushing to his feet. His curly hair bounces over the freckles on his nose as he does so.

"Sorry. Gotta go. Sorry!" he stammers quickly before kicking into a sprint toward the gas station.

She frowns, realizing that the crash wasn't her fault, after all. That boy had been running and bumped into her. Why does she always assume things were her fault? It certainly isn't an enjoyable way to live, and clearly this mopey attitude isn't winning her any friends. She's chased away two good ones already.

Maybe it's time to change her outlook.

She climbs to her feet, and as she dusts herself off, two large men come barreling down the sidewalk toward her. This time, she's going to get out of their way.

But they slow to a stop as they approach.

"Excuse me, miss, did you see a boy run by here?" asks one of them. Neither of the men is panting or even breaking a sweat as they await her reply, staring at her behind dark sunglasses.

So that boy wasn't just running. He was being chased.

She wonders what he did. These two men seem like authority figures of some kind, though she notices no insignia or uniform outside their simple black suits.

Whatever the reason, she feels no guilt in being honest. After all, the kid had knocked her over and took off without bothering to help her. She's getting tired of being pushed around. How much longer is she going to keep letting it happen? And if these guys are after him, he probably did something to deserve it.

"Yes, he went right around the gas station," she says, happy to tell the truth of her own free will for once. Every other time she'd ratted someone out, it had been because of her inability to lie. She always prefers to cover for people. Not this time.

The two men nod at each other before taking off in that direction.

Amazingly, the clouds hold their rain at bay long enough for her to reach the orphanage. And when Sister Agatha sends her outside to trim the hedges that border the property wall, the clouds even part a smidge to allow a bit of warm sunlight to shine on her as she works. Maybe things are looking up, after all.

When she finishes her chores for the day, Brielle joins the other children for dinner, promising herself that she's not going to take any guff from anyone this evening. This is the beginning of a new Brielle, and she's determined to keep it that way.

Luckily, no one teases her through dinner, although she almost wishes they would so she could practice standing up for herself. Just because she had to be honest all the time didn't mean she had to let others mess with her.

After dinner, she decided to join the small crowd in the living room. It was Sister Agatha's routine to watch an hour of television before lights out, and any of the children are always free to join her, so long as they remained silent and respectful.

Tonight, the local news seemed to be what piqued the nun's fancy. Brielle pretzels her legs as she sits on the carpet at the foot of Sister Agatha's arm chair, surprisingly satisfied with how the day had turned out. She's still friendless, but no longer miserable about it.

A face appears on the screen as Brielle makes herself comfortable, and immediately, those efforts are made impossible, as every muscle in her body tightens on edge.

The face is of a teenage boy with curly brown hair and

freckles on his nose. The boy who knocked her down earlier today!

She leans closer to the box television as she strains to hear every word the news anchor is saying.

"This evening, the body of Malachi Jones was found in a dumpster behind the Gas N' Go," the male reporter says as the face shrinks into a square to the left of the handsome anchor's head. "Malachi had gone missing three years ago, though there've been reports of him hosting a sort of shanty town for runaways like him. As of yet, there have been no anonymous tips as to how he ended up in this dumpster, but FBI Agent Jack Cadbury is currently on the scene to investigate…"

The screen changes to show the area in real time, a balding middle-aged man in a suit looking slightly forlorn as he talks to police deputies.

"Malachi was one of our informants," the FBI agent explains to the camera when they finally get his attention. "All I can say is that he was investigating some potentially threatening individuals, and I can only imagine they were the cause of his death…"

Brielle can feel that her face has completely drained of blood. Terror floods her limbs, making them feel cold and numb at the same time.

Oh no! There's not a single shred of doubt in her mind that he's the same boy she ran into earlier—the same boy she willfully ratted out on.

She's the reason he's dead!

It can't just be coincidence that those men were chasing him, and his body is being found on the local news. If she hadn't told those men where he'd gone, they might not have ever found him.

No, no, no! She really is a terrible person. She'd been so wrong earlier, so proud of her decision to tattle on him, all because he'd knocked her over in what she now realizes was a desperate flight to escape men who were trying to murder him! How could she have been so foolish, so selfish!

A boy's death is on her hands. How is she ever going to get past this?

The air is silent and still in the car as they head for the meeting place. When Brielle sneaks a sideways glance at Tristan, his whole body looks tense. His jaw is clenched, his biceps are bulging in the blue sleeves of his t-shirt, and his knuckles are white as his fingers grip the steering wheel.

This is the first time the two of them have really been alone since the whole Ada-is-the-missing-Gemini fiasco, and she has no idea what to say to him or how to act in his presence. It feels like she's constantly fighting the urge to fidget with this or that body part.

When did things get so weird between them?

Then again, have things between them ever not been weird?

"So, where are we supposed to meet Jack?" Brielle asks. She remembers the location, but she can't stand the silence.

"The Gas N' Go on Main Street," Tristan replies, the tone of his voice sounding like he's glad for an icebreaker.

She knew that place well. She used to pass it every day on her way to the orphanage from school growing up. Before that whole thing with the boy she'd run into.

Malachi.

She'd never forget his name. It was her fault that he was dead.

She had taken a different route home after that, and kept the same route every day for years since. She couldn't bear to walk by it, haunted by the memory of it every time she did.

And though she was older and wiser now, blessed to be a Zodiac Guardian with powers and a destiny to save the Universe, the knowledge that she had to go there once again weighs heavily on her.

Why couldn't Jack have chosen any other location?

Tristan clears his throat. "You know, I never felt anything for Ada." His eyes are trained on the road, not daring to flicker in her direction. "Not even after I believed she was..." He can't bring himself to say the word.

"It's okay, Tristan," she says immediately. "You really don't have to—"

"No, I do," he interrupts, his eyes closing for a moment. "I..." He bites his lower lip, and she can sense an anger rising in him. He turns to her suddenly. "I didn't choose to end things between us. If I had my way, you and I—"

Now it's her turn to interrupt him. "To what end?"

His lips snap shut on what she knew he was going to say.

She looks out the window, unable to bear seeing his face. Why did he have to address this now?

"You'll find her eventually, and it will just hurt all over again," she explains, fighting the tears that well in her eyes. "It's better for us to not be."

Tristan says nothing, and the tension returns tenfold as they drive the rest of the short trip in silence. She pulls out her phone before they pull in, seeing that still no texts have come from Kerrim. She needs him. Needs a buffer from her feelings for Tristan. When Kerrim is around, flirting and... other things...she can forget about Tristan for fleeting moments.

She needs Kerrim now more than ever. But still, nothing.

They pull into the gas station, and the mood in the truck slowly shifts from awkward sexual tension to dark anxiety.

Jack is leaning against his gray sedan parked behind the gas station, exhaling smoke as he lowers his cigarette down to his waist, seeing them approach. Apparently, he recognizes Tristan's truck—committed it to memory is more like it.

As they park, Brielle sees him drop his cigarette and step on it. She can't help but wonder how Logan got him to agree to this meeting. She knows Logan keeps much from him, as does Veronica. And she appreciates the fact that Logan is putting a lot on the line in doing this. Does Jack trust Logan still? Knowing he's, at the very least, acquainted with his number-one most-wanted?

If only Jack knew how wrong he is in villainizing Tristan.

Tristan pulls the key out of the ignition and steps out, and Brielle follows behind him.

"Ayers," Jack regards him as he approaches.

"Cadbury," Tristan greets solemnly, though with a slight lift in the corner of his lips.

Jack crosses his arms. "Cut to the chase. What do you want?"

Tristan leans against the bed of his truck, copying Jack's stance. She wishes he didn't feel the need to mock him like this, despite whatever weird rivalry the two have. They need Jack to be complacent. It might have been better if Tristan hadn't come, but then again, if he hadn't, she's pretty sure Jack wouldn't have agreed to this rendezvous.

"Your team recently found a book that's of great importance to us," Tristan says, all signs of taunting gone. "We're not asking to obtain it from you, but merely for an opportunity to look at it."

Jack doesn't break his stare from Tristan's face, or move in any way to suggest he'd heard what Tristan said. He might as well have been deaf to Tristan for all Brielle saw.

Tristan sighs and lowers his head for a moment. "Look, I know you think I'm the bad guy, but I can assure you that I'm the one trying to protect you, and everyone else, from the true villain. And all I need to do is to see what's in that book."

The book that supposedly tells of a ship out in space that houses thousands, if not more, of refugees from Chardis's initial attack on Gemini I.

Jack looks away, his fingers fidgeting as if he wishes there was another cigarette between them. "I have no desire to help you, Ayers." He hangs his head. "I don't know what Logan sees in you, or Veronica, or any of your lackeys for that matter." He juts his chin at Brielle. "But I have no intention of making any further deals with you."

Tristan opens his mouth to speak, but Jack raises a silencing hand and steps away from his car, beginning to pace as he clasps his hands behind his back. "Do you know what happened at this very gas station?"

Tristan barely has a chance to shake his head before Jack continues. "No, of course you don't. You never seem to notice when your influence harms others. Six years ago, a boy named Malachi, a boy who just beforehand was seen canoodling with you, was murdered."

The name stabs through Brielle's chest, knocking the breath from her lungs, and she has to grip the top of the bed to keep from crumpling.

"Malachi?" Tristan seems to play with the name on his tongue, unsure of where he's heard it before.

Jack nods. "He was one of my informants, investigating a girl I believed to be a threat, the girl who's now known as Dyad."

This name has Tristan's head shooting up, and, too late, he tries to hide his reaction.

"See, I knew you'd remember," Jack continues accusingly, stopping in his pacing to glare at Tristan. "That was right when you turned up, and days later, Malachi was dead. His body carelessly tossed into a dumpster. By you!"

"No!" Brielle shouts just seconds after Tristan turns argumentative eyes on Jack, prepared to defend himself.

Now both of them look at Brielle, and her throat constricts with the confession she's been holding back for six years.

She shakes her head and squeezes her eyes shut. "Tristan had nothing to do with Malachi's death. But I did."

When she dares to open her eyes, she sees them both looking at her quizzically, albeit for different reasons. She lowers her head.

"I didn't even know Tristan then, didn't know anything," she begins, staring guiltily down at her feet. "I was eleven, walking home from school, and this random boy ran into me, then ran off, right near here. A few minutes later, two men came by asking if I'd seen him and—" her throat muscles constrict, making it impossible for her to continue. She swallows down the lump. "I told them where he went, and...that night I saw the news report about his murder..."

She tentatively glances up at the two men, finding them both staring at her. Tristan with pity and understanding, and Jack with a mask. She can't tell if he's judging her or just doesn't believe her.

Again, Tristan opens his mouth to say something, but Jack cuts him off.

"It doesn't matter." Jack casts a stern look down at the pavement, then raises his eyes to glare at them. "These are my terms, take it or leave it." He pauses for dramatic effect, perhaps making sure they're listening. "I know you know who Dyad is, and his whereabouts. If you want the book, I want Dyad. Period."

Tristan's face goes blank, as does Brielle's, and Jack rounds his car to hop into the driver's seat. She sees the glow of his lighter sparking before he pulls out and drives away.

Great. Now what are they going to do?

20

ADA

"What are you looking at?" Jareth asks Ada, wheeling over from his computer to hers.

Ada looks up in surprise. She'd been so absorbed with what she's doing that she'd forgotten she was in a room with most of the other Zodiacs. "Oh. I'm trying to hack into a satellite."

Cassandra's head snaps up. "You're what?"

"Ada's trying to commandeer a satellite for our own use," Esther explains. "So we can observe what's on the other side of the wormhole."

Cassandra's eyes widen as she wheels over, too. "Wow. I was cruising images of planets seeing if I could find anything that looked like what Tristan saw. This is a much better idea."

Logan stands up and walks to stand beside her, shaking his head ruefully. "Except we don't know how to do that."

Jareth wipes his hand down his face. "I'd never done so many illegal things until I became a Zodiac."

Ada flashes him a grin. "Then you haven't lived."

She turns back to her computer and notes the lines of

data that just filled the screen. She taps a few keys, eyes narrowing in focus. NASA's firewall is impressive.

But, hey, she likes a challenge.

"So?" Cassandra asks. "Is it working? Are we going to have our very own satellite?"

Ada blinks, having already lost herself to the world of encryption and decryption. "Ah, I'm not sure yet."

Eric moves away from the computer closest to the door. Ada noticed that's the one he chose. The one furthest from her. And nearest the exit. Giving him space is the hardest thing she's ever done, but she's determined to take this at his pace.

For once, Eric is going to call the shots.

Even if it kills her.

He steps past Cassandra and stops near Ada. "She'll concentrate better if you just let her focus."

She smiles up at him gratefully. He knows her so well. How many hours has he sat beside her, reading something, while she steadily chipped away at some corporation's digital defenses?

Eric's lips twitch before he quickly looks away. The action has both hope and hurt flashing through her. His natural inclination was to smile right back at her, just like it always has been. There's a part of Eric that still loves her. She knows it.

But he suppressed that part. He looked away. A bigger part of Eric is still hurting.

Ada turns back to her computer, fingernails digging into her palms. This is how she can show Eric that she respects and understands his choices. That there's nothing she wouldn't do for him.

Drawing in a steadying breath, she scans the new data that just appeared on her screen. "Wow," she breathes. "We're past the first firewall."

"Oo—" Cassandra quickly cuts herself off. "This is cool," she whispers.

Eric shuffles closer and squats down. "My guess is they have a threat management firewall?"

Ada nods as she types. "Yep, far more than the usual packet-filtering ones. Which is why I'm convincing them I'm not a threat."

"That's my gir—"

Ada continues typing even as Eric catches himself. He's always called her his girl. Always been proud of what she can do.

They just have to get back there again.

Lines of data pour down the screen like a waterfall.

"Is that good?" Cassandra asks in a hushed voice.

Eric grins. "Ada's past the second gatekeeper."

"One more to go," she mutters determinedly.

The sound of footsteps coming down the stairs tells Ada that Tristan and Brielle are back. Everyone else turns around but her. She just needs to get past the DPI...

"Did you get the book?" Jareth asks.

"No," Tristan says heavily. "I didn't really expect him to just hand it over, to be honest."

"What did he say?" This time it's Logan asking the question, his voice a little heavier. This is his father they're talking about.

"That he has no intention of handing the book over," says Tristan flatly.

"Hey," says Veronica, sounding suspicious. "What was that look between the two of you?"

Ada almost turns around, curious that something just passed between Tristan and Brielle. But then the data streaming starts again. She's almost there...

"We learned something about a kid we used to know," says Tristan. "It's not important right now."

Ada doesn't need Brielle's lie detecting ability to hear that Tristan is hedging. She's about to turn around when two words appear on her screen.

Access granted.

She lets out a whoop of victory. "We have ourselves a satellite!"

"No way!" exclaims Cassandra as she rushes back.

Ada turns, only one person she's looking for. One person who she wants to celebrate with. Eric was already striding back toward her, a heart-stopping grin lighting up his handsome face. He stops as if he realized what he was doing, then seems to stand there in suspended animation, uncertain of his next move.

Come and revel in this moment with me, she pleads internally.

But Eric stays where he is. He smiles warmly. "I never doubted you for a second."

Ada blinks, knowing that's the truth, but desperately wanting his arms around her. A flash of what life might be like if this is as far as Eric can bring himself to trust her stabs like a white-hot knife. He'll always be close by, always a friend, but never anything more.

And she'll have to convince herself it's enough.

Always hoping he'll want more...

Ada turns back to her computer, knowing it would be torture, a life of constant yearning, but it's a life with Eric in it. She's not willing to contemplate anything else.

Tristan appears beside her. "You've hacked into a satellite?"

"Sure have," she says, trying to find her earlier excitement. "To send through the wormhole."

"That's genius," he says, clearly impressed.

She shrugs, liking the praise, but still subdued because it's Eric's recognition that she really wanted. Further proof that a future is hollow without him. "We need to find out what's on the other side," she says, trying to get her head back in the game.

"So, we're doing this?" asks Cassandra, clearly just as excited and impressed as Tristan is.

Ada lets out a slow breath. "We're doing this."

Her fingers fly over the keyboard once more as she takes over the satellite's controls and enters the coordinates for the wormhole. That done, she projects the image the satellite is recording onto the large screen before them.

It flickers before the blackness of space fills it, the body of the satellite in the foreground, stars dotted beyond. Ada sits back as the satellite begins to move, following its new trajectory. "Atta girl."

Veronica lets out a low whistle. "So cool."

Everyone moves in a little closer as they watch the slow-moving machine move through the vacuum of space.

Jareth draws in a sharp breath. "Is that it?"

A ripple can be seen ahead, distorting the smooth inky nothingness they're in. The blackness dotted with stars is warped and curved, almost looking like the smooth lip of a cliff.

"Yep, that's it," says Ada, unsure if she's breathing. "A giant sinkhole in space."

"That connects to another point in space," adds Eric.

"So, just to make sure I've got this straight," says Logan, his voice tense. "A wormhole is essentially a tunnel, each end at a separate place in the universe."

Ada nods, not taking her gaze off the screen. "Yes. A shortcut of sorts. As if space has been folded, meaning the other side could be billions of lightyears away, but would only take a few seconds to traverse."

"Mind. Blown," mutters Cassandra.

Suddenly, the satellite picks up pace, zooming forward.

Eric leans in, looking over Ada's shoulder. "It's approaching the event horizon."

"Event horizon?" asks Brielle.

Ada nods, barely blinking. "The point of no return. Gravity is progressively multiplying the closer the satellite gets to the mouth of the wormhole. There will be a point where nothing can stop it from being sucked in—the event horizon."

Which is exactly what will happen to them if they follow the path the satellite is forging.

The satellite begins to move faster and faster, the stars around it blurring.

With a short, sharp movement, it changes angle, tilting as if it just fell down a well.

Or a wormhole.

Before Ada can blink, it's flying faster than anything she's ever seen. Streaks of light zoom past, like an exploding meteor shower. The image shakes, as does the body of the satellite in the foreground. Ada half expects pieces to start flying off.

Or for it to collapse like a soda can.

Please make it through.

The streaks become lines, variegating the black with blinding white. It's beautiful. Dazzling. Breathtaking and hypnotizing.

The light show has barely started when everything goes black.

Everyone in the room, the very air itself, holds its breath. Time stands still as they wait to see if the satellite made it.

If passing through is even possible.

The screen stares back at them, as if unsure what they're waiting for.

Ada's eyes scan the black frantically, looking for something, anything, that may indicate they're on the other side.

There's a flicker of light and a chorus of gasps moves through the Zodiacs. Suddenly, an image large enough to have them all drawing back in shock appears. It's far bigger than any of them expected.

And far more impressive.

A planet dominates the screen, spherical and the most radiant blue Ada's ever seen. Cerulean, cobalt, azure and sapphire all swirl in intricate patterns over the surface, giving it a liquid, ethereal look. Two rings of pure white circle it, spinning in opposite directions.

Tristan gasps. "That's the planet from my vision."

Ada's knees go weak. The one that is possibly destroyed, along with every living being on it.

"Esther?" Ada asks, her voice raspy. "Can we identify it?"

"Yes, Ada. Alden left an extensive amount of information and data on the universe we inhabit."

For once, even Ada's feeling a little frustrated with Esther being so literal. She's going to have to do something about her programming. "And? What planet is this?"

"It is the home planet of the Aquarius people," Esther states calmly. As if the news didn't just rock the room. "Known as Aqua."

Ada turns to Eric, stunned.

The planet they're looking at, the one potentially fated to be destroyed, is his home planet.

21

ERIC

The entire world falls away as Eric stares unblinkingly at the image on the large flat screen. The planet looks so completely foreign, with its vast expanse of bright blue ocean covering most of what can be seen on this side, only a dash of the one land mass visible off to the left. It looks like a ripe blueberry. Nothing like the satellite images he's seen of Earth. And yet, he imagines that astronauts feel this same gut-wrenching awe when they see Earth from space for the first time.

This is his home planet. The world he'd have grown up on, been a prince of, if Chardis hadn't ruined everything.

A thousand questions flood into his mind. Are his real parents still alive? Are they on that planet right now? What do they look like? Do they miss him?

Through that white noise whispers a realization that he's not yet ready to hear. The truth it promises is too awful to fathom.

"That's the planet from my vision," Tristan says solemnly, voicing the very knowledge Eric has been rejecting. He feels Tristan's eyes turn to him. "I'm sorry, Eric."

Sorrow plunges through Eric's gut, as if Tristan had stabbed him with a knife rather than spoken a handful of words.

This planet—*his* planet—is the one Tristan saw get destroyed in his vision. Eric has finally laid eyes on the home he never dared to dream he'd see again, and just as that hope began to explode within him, it got taken away forever. The family he never got to meet is going to die at Chardis's hands, and there's nothing Eric can do to stop it.

Before anyone can see the tears springing down his cheeks, he dashes out of HQ and up the stairs to the room that's been his for the last few days. He closes the door and leans against it as the hot tears burn his cheeks. A sudden fury fills him, and he's seized with the urge to break something, to unleash this rage that threatens to devour him and make something just as damaged as he feels.

But looking around the room, he realizes that none of these things are his. He has no right to smash anything, no right to punch a hole into any of the walls or slam his foot through the wood of the door that's barely holding him up.

Doing the only thing he can think of, he pulls his shirt up over his head. The tremors rippling through his body steal the accuracy from his fingers, making the gesture take longer, which only increases his frustration. When he finally has the damn thing in his hands, he digs into the light blue fabric and rips it apart, over and over again until there's nothing but shreds and frayed strings strewn around him like sad confetti.

Then he storms to the bed and throws himself onto it, howling all his rage into the pillow he's trying to smother himself with.

The expulsion of all that emotion has left him completely spent, and he just lays there, facedown, feeling completely and absolutely helpless.

He has nothing. He's lost the family he should've had. He lost Ada. He's about to lose his home world. And he's just destroyed one of the only true possessions he had—his damn shirt.

What was the point of any of this? He and Ada had spent their lives trying to figure out who they were. And for what? The truth they uncovered didn't bring them any closer to anything, and had only yanked them apart. Now, he wishes more than anything that he didn't know about any of this. Didn't know about the Zodiacs, about Chardis, about his planet.

Why couldn't they have just stayed blissfully ignorant and led a happy life together? Why couldn't they have let well enough alone?

A soft rapping knocks on the door, and he doesn't have to look up from his safety pillow to know who it is. He hears the doorknob turn and the door open slightly.

"Eric, can I come in?" Ada asks in a soft voice. It's filled with so much concern and love that the sound threatens to finish him off. Put a fork in him, he's done.

He can't answer, so when he doesn't tell her no, she takes his silence as a yes, and the sound of light footsteps comes closer until he feels her weight settle on the bed beside him.

She doesn't say anything for a moment, just sits there, perhaps expecting him to sit up and look at her. But he can't. With the anger expelled, he's left with nothing but the heavy grief, and it's like lead filling every one of his limbs, pinning him to the spot.

After a while, she gently sets her hand on his bare back, and the feeling of her flesh directly on his sends a shiver through him. It's warm and loving, with just the slightest hint of her static energy, and every inch of him tries to soak it up like a dry sponge to a raindrop.

"Everything is going to be okay, Eric," she promises, her voice like a feather caressing his eardrum.

He doesn't believe the words, but he needs to hear them, or any words, so long as they're from her lips. Her voice is like a tether, holding him dangling just above the pit of despair that means to swallow him.

"Tristan didn't just have the one vision of your planet being destroyed," she continues after a moment, and her thumb begins to gently stroke over the ridge of his shoulder blade. "His visions always come in pairs, two eventualities. The other half of his vision was that we save your world, by working together."

"How?" The word bubbles out of him, and he's not sure she can even hear it through the pillow.

She sighs. "I don't know, but I promise you that we will do everything in our power to save Aqua. *I* will do whatever it takes to save your home. I won't ever let you be alone."

He savors her promise, feeling the love she still has for him. The love he will always have for her.

That love gives him the will to roll over just enough so he can look at and see her face. "How can we possibly accomplish saving Aqua?" he asks, his voice deep and breaking. "We don't have a spaceship with which to get there. And even if we did, we don't know for certain how stable that wormhole is. Just because we got a satellite to pass through unharmed doesn't mean the same would be true for us. And, even if we make it through, how can we possibly stand against Chardis's space armada?"

He gets more and more defeated with each word he says, convincing himself even further that there truly is no hope.

"We'll find a way, Eric," she coos. "We always do. You just need to have faith." Her expression changes, becoming more firm. "But I can't do it without you. I'll need your help with the tech. You can't give up before we even start. That's not the Eric I know."

That statement is like a wakeup slap to his heart. He knows she's right. If they're going to have even a snowball's chance in hell at saving his home planet, he can't mope around in bed forever.

Just as he's about to muster up the will to sit up, she climbs onto the bed to lay beside him, and suddenly, there's nowhere else he'd rather be. Her head is on the pillow only inches away from his, her beautiful face so close he can smell her sweet breath.

For a long time, they don't say anything, don't touch. They just stare into each other's eyes. He wants to tell her that he loves her, that he's done pushing away, that he needs her now more than ever.

But he doesn't.

For now, this is enough.

BRIELLE

"How are we going to get through that wormhole?" Logan asks the question they're all thinking.

Brielle can't imagine what Eric's feeling right now, wherever he ran off to. He'd stormed off as soon as he realized what the image on the screen meant. What if it was her planet that was about to be attacked by Chardis? She couldn't even fathom what it would be like to see it, let alone to know it might be destroyed and she'd never have a chance to visit it in person.

Of course Eric is devastated.

But that destruction isn't a certainty. As always with Tristan's visions, they have to hope that the preferable outcome is the true one. Which means they have to find a way through that wormhole.

"Can't we just go through in our suits?" Cassandra asks, jutting out her hip as she looks around at the others for verification.

Tristan shakes his head. "I'm no astrophysicist, but I think that would be too risky. Wormholes shrink and compress the matter that passes through them. We have no idea what such compression would do to us if we try to go through without more protection."

"But the satellite made it through just fine," Brielle points out. "And so did that Earth-killer asteroid a few weeks ago."

"Yes, but they weren't living things," Tristan counters, tapping his foot as he sits back in the spinney desk chair. "We can't be certain what the pressure of the event horizon will do to a beating heart, or any other vital organs. It's just too risky to charge in without being fully prepared, without knowing exactly what will happen."

"Do we have time to figure it out?" It's Veronica who asks the question, clinging to one of Jareth's arms. "Was there anything in your vision to hint at when Chardis will attack the planet?"

Tristan's head lowers as he shakes it back and forth.

"Veronica's right, we can't just wait around for an answer to fall into our laps," Cassandra says, flipping a stray blonde lock over her shoulder, her attitude coming out. "Chardis could attack tomorrow for all we know, and we can't be too afraid to take action."

"At this time, I detect no foreign object around Aqua," Esther informs them through the speakers. "I will continue to monitor the area around the planet within the radius of one astronomical unit and alert you when anything enters that space."

"I'm sorry, what's an astro-whatever-you-said?" Veronica asks, frowning in confusion.

"One hundred and fifty thousand kilometers, or just over ninety thousand miles," Esther informs.

"Whoa," Cassandra hisses. "Esther, you're amazing!"

"Thank you, Cassandra," Esther replies without emotion.

Brielle is a little stunned. She had no idea Esther could do that, all from just satellite access. Ada really is a genius.

"That's about the same number of miles on my car,

Sunshine," Jareth says with wide eyes. "It took me over a decade to put those miles on. Granted a spaceship will be able to go much faster, but still, that gives us some warning."

"So, what do we do in the meantime?" Brielle asks. "How can we possibly prepare to stop an armada?"

Tristan sits up then and faces the screen. "Esther, can you send Aqua a message from the satellite? Maybe we can at least warn them that Chardis is coming."

Esther doesn't respond right away, perhaps calculating a response to Tristan's question. "I will have to monitor the outgoing signals from the planet to decipher their language. At the same time, I will attempt to mimic the frequencies they use with the inferior technology on the satellite. It will take approximately sixty-two hours."

Tristan puts his hands up behind his head and sighs, seeming to be unsure how he feels about this time-frame. "We'll just have to hope that's long enough. Thank you, Esther."

"You're welcome, Tristan."

"Okay, so we send them a warning," Cassandra begins. "But that's not good enough. Your vision showed *us* being there. Which means the only way to save Aqua is for us to physically get through that wormhole." She cocks her head at him. "Doesn't you seeing us there mean that we can safely cross?"

"Maybe, but the vision didn't show me how we got there," Tristan explains, his frustration clear in his gruff tone and elevating pitch. He sighs again. "Let's take a break and clear our heads. Maybe we'll come up with something after some fresh air."

As the group disperses, Brielle's phone dings. She pulls it out of her pocket, and her heart leaps into her throat.

It's a text from Kerrim!

"Hey, sorry for being MIA the last few days. Wanna grab lunch at the diner?"

She doesn't even bother to hide her enthusiasm from him. He's exactly the distraction she needs right now. *"Sure! I'll be right over."*

She walks toward the door, but Tristan heads her off. "Hey, you wanna grab a bite?"

Uh oh...

"Umm, actually, I'm meeting Kerrim for lunch," she says, avoiding meeting his eyes. "Maybe some other time."

"Oh... Okay." He steps out of her way and goes back to sit at the desk chair.

She hates sensing his dejection, but she can't worry about that right now. She spends way too much time worrying about what Tristan is thinking and feeling, and she can't live her entire life like that. And she doesn't want to keep Kerrim waiting.

Even though he's kept her waiting for days.

She skips out and rides her bike to the diner.

Kerrim is already sitting in their usual booth when she gets there. When he sees her walk in, his lips quirk up in that sexy smile, and her insides churn.

She's tempted to suggest that they skip the meal and go straight to making out in his car, but she doesn't want to make it easy for him. She deserves an explanation as to why he ghosted her.

She slides into the booth across from him and cuts right to the chase. "So, where have you been the last few days?" Beating around the bush has never been her strong suit, the whole not-being-able-to-lie thing and all.

He hangs his head, wearing a rueful smile. "I know, I'm sorry. I had to go to D.C. to help my dad with a business matter. I wanted to text you, but I didn't have good cell service. I hope you don't hate me."

Her lie alarm didn't go off. He was telling the truth.

"Not completely," she teases, relieved that he wasn't just being a typical jerk guy.

He leans forward and arches a sexy brow, his eyes sparking with dark promise as they lock onto hers. "I'm sure I can make it up to you."

Heat flushes up her neck and her mouth goes suddenly dry. He seems to appreciate the blush in her cheeks, his teeth scraping his bottom lip in a way that makes her want to bite it, too.

Yes, he's exactly what she needs right now, and again, she's tempted to get up and tug him to his car. But the growling in her stomach reminds her that all she's eaten today was a piece of toast with jam on it. She won't be any good to anyone if she doesn't get more food in her. She'll just make sure not to order anything with garlic.

They get their food and enjoy a fun, flirtatious meal, their conversation riddled with innuendo, and she can't wait to finish and get to dessert.

Just as the check comes and her anticipation accomplished turning her insides into a tight knot, her watch flashes orange.

No, not now!

She reluctantly taps the small screen. *"Meet at Tristan's ASAP."*

Has Chardis come already? No, the alert was only orange. She's certain that it would've been red if the attack was coming. Either way, she's not going to get dessert right now.

"Shall we go somewhere more private?" Kerrim asks, creeping his hand across the table toward hers.

Groaning softly in the back of her throat, she pulls her hand back and stands up. "Unfortunately, I have to go. My friends need me. But soon, I promise."

He frowns as he stands as well, still managing to look

completely edible. "Okay," he sighs. "But you owe me." He winks, and she just about melts.

She nods and makes to turn for the entrance, but he grabs her hand and pulls her into him, pressing his lips against hers, and she does melt, opening her mouth to get a taste of him.

Before she can completely dissolve under his tongue, she breaks away and rushes for the door.

"This better be good," she mutters.

23

TRISTAN

Tristan's jaw hasn't unwound since Brielle left HQ.

To be with that douche bag, Kerrim.

He glances down at the carpet beneath him, surprised his pacing hasn't worn a groove in it. He spins and prowls back to his computer, his teeth grinding in frustration.

Of all the guys Brielle could've hooked up with, it had to be Kerrim. He doesn't like the guy. Doesn't trust him.

In fact, just thinking of him has Tristan's hands clenching into fists. Fists that he's already imagining ploughing into the guy's smug-assed face.

"Can you use that restless energy to go grab me a soda?" says Ada from where she's still parked beside her computer.

Tristan sighs. Seems she's back in the land of the living.

While everyone else has left to get something to eat, Ada's been deeply absorbed in analyzing the data coming from the satellite, trying to find out whether they could pass through the wormhole.

To save Eric's planet.

"Anything?" asks Tristan.

Ada sighs. "Not yet. There are just so many variables we don't know once we pass the event horizon."

"The speed of entrance," adds Esther. "The multiplying gravity. The radial size of the event horizon itself. Whether the suits can resist spaghettification—"

Tristan raises a hand. "I get the idea." The thought of any of the Zodiacs turning to pasta makes him ill.

Deciding how they're going to save Aqua is the biggest decision he's had to make so far.

Ada leans back, stretching her arms above her head with a soft groan. "I'm going to need some caffeine or something. Preferably carbonated."

Glad for something to do, no matter how small it is, Tristan turns toward the door, only to find Eric entering.

He lifts up the tray he's holding. "I brought you two a couple of colas and some sandwiches."

Ada beams and Tristan's chest tightens. Those two are meant to be together. Although he understands that Eric was hurt, if there was nothing keeping him and Brielle apart... well, she definitely would not be with a douchebag, smug-assed guy right now.

Eric sits the plate with the sandwiches—each cut into little triangles—and the sodas on a nearby table. Ada stands up and stretches again. "You're a lifesaver," she says warmly.

Eric's cheeks flush, but he doesn't answer.

Ada glances down at her rumpled clothing. "Actually, I might take a quick shower and get some fresh clothes on," she says, her nose wrinkling. "Esther's scanning the data that's coming through the wormhole. Hopefully it will give us some answers."

Eric nods, but once again doesn't reply. Ada's smile wavers but she quickly pulls it back up, glancing between Eric and Tristan before jogging up the stairs.

Tristan watches her leave. "She really loves you, you know," he says, turning back to Eric.

He winces. "And I thought that was enough."

"If you two could be proof that in some cases it is, I'd really appreciate it."

Eric stills, no doubt knowing what Tristan's talking about. He and Brielle's feelings are the strongest, realest thing Tristan's ever experienced.

And yet, it won't ever be enough. Not when fate has other plans for him.

Eric lets out a long breath and sits heavily on the nearest chair. "I wish it were that simple."

"Ada made a mistake," Tristan points out. "And a well-meaning one, at that."

Eric's gaze snaps to his, a deep, simmering mix of pain and anger brewing in there. "Aren't most mistakes well-meaning? And does that make them hurt any less?"

Compassion has Tristan nodding. Pain is pain, no matter how it was inflicted.

"I need to know I'll never feel anything like that again," Eric says hoarsely, the echoes of the agony he experienced when he thought he'd lost Ada rippling through the room. He frowns, the anger blazing again. "Would you risk it?"

Tristan's own pain claws at his heart. "I was going to. I was about to tell Brielle how I felt, but she broke it off." That moment in Creamy Dreams is forever branded in his mind.

"Do you regret it?" asks Eric, watching him closely.

Tristan sighs. Would he have still kissed Brielle, almost told her how he really feels, if he knew what it meant for them now? That all the pain and awkwardness and wishing it could've been more than a fleeting moment in time would've been avoided?

Yes, he would. He'd do it again.

Because those moments are the moments they're fighting

for. The beauty of life. The reason to breathe, no matter how much it hurts.

"No, I don't regret it," he says softly. "Despite it all, I'd do it again."

Somehow, Eric looks surprised and unsurprised all at once. Like the words have struck a chord, but he kind of wishes it didn't.

Tristan walks over and places a hand on Eric's shoulder. "Nothing can protect you from pain, not even your powers. So, the question you need to ask yourself, is avoiding that worth losing what you had with Ada?" Eric blinks, but Tristan isn't finished. The Aquarius in their team needs to realize what he's risking. "And what if you were to lose her forever?"

Kind of like Brielle can never be Tristan's.

Pain, far sharper and deeper than Tristan's seen, flashes through Eric's eyes. He swallows. Blinks. Then swallows again.

It's possible he took what they have for granted in the same way she did. That the pain of impulsive, well-meaning choices is nothing compared to the prospect of loss.

Eric pushes to his feet and Tristan's hand slips away, knowing he's given him a lot to think about.

Ada appears in the entrance, looking bright and fresh in a clean t-shirt and jeans. She glances between Tristan and Eric, seeming to realize they'd just had a deep and meaningful conversation. "Is everything okay?"

"Hopefully, it will be soon," Tristan says jovially.

Ada's gaze returns to Eric, hope shimmers in the depths. "Eric?" she whispers. The yearning in her voice is unmistakable.

Tristan quietly makes his way past her, holding his breath, but Esther's voice interrupts the tension that had thickened the air. "Tristan. I would advise you to remain in the room."

He turns around, unease creeping up his spine despite Esther's usual calm tone. "Because?"

"Because I've detected a significant change in dark matter at a location within the subway system."

A map appears on the large screen, showing a pulsing black dot only a few miles from here.

It's either Skins.

Or another Zodiac.

Every muscle in Tristan's body coils in preparation. "Esther, call the Zodiacs. We're rolling out."

24

ADA

The subway section that Esther leads them to is cordoned off for maintenance. It means it's eerily quiet as the Zodiacs come down the stairs and fan out.

Ada can feel electricity tingling over the tips of her fingers as she scans left then right. The back wall is covered in soot, charred posters peeling off. Paint tins sit beside it, with scaffolding along the wall and thick sheets covering much of the tiled floor.

Except there aren't any painters.

"At least there are no bystanders," Jareth mutters.

The last thing they need right now is more publicity for the Zodiacs.

"And so far, so good—no Skins," adds Cassandra.

Tristan nods, looking as if he's a giant ball of kinetic energy just waiting to detonate. "Something or someone is here," he says in a low voice. "We need to find them."

A few more steps and they're in a line along the platform, a silent breeze blowing through the tunnel.

"Hello?" They all tense at the tentative voice. A young woman steps around the scaffolding, shoulders hunched and arms crossed, tears streaking down her face. "Is someone there?"

She pulls up when she sees seven people on the other side of the platform. "Oh."

"Are you okay?" Tristan asks, although he doesn't move.

"I…" The young woman hunches her shoulders even more. "I don't think so."

Eric's hands twitch by his side. "Are you hurt?"

Of course Eric would be the one to ask that. He's the one who can take the girl's pain away.

The girl shakes her head. "No." Her lower lip trembles. "I can't help but keep coming back." She indicates with her chin toward the burned wall. "To see what I've done."

Ada senses the collective gasp from the other Zodiacs. Have they found another one?

Cassandra arches an eyebrow. "Looks like something I'd do."

The girl seems to brighten at that. "You have…abilities, too?" she asks, her voice hushed.

"We all do," says Tristan, but Ada notices he hasn't moved. For some reason, he's holding back.

The girl takes a couple of steps closer, her footsteps silent on the covered floor. "You do? You can…make fire?"

Brielle takes two steps forward, but Tristan shoots out a hand and stops her. She looks back at him. It seems they've found another Zodiac.

Except he shakes his head imperceptibly. "I don't remember anything about a Zodiac having that sort of power."

Ada frowns. In fact, fire can't exist in the vacuum of space.

The girl hears him because her brow instantly contracts. A moment later, her chin snaps up and her lip curls in a snarl. "I'd never want to be one of you," she spits.

Her hands appear from where they'd been tucked. She smiles as she reveals the two revolvers she's holding.

Three things happen simultaneously.

Tristan shouts, "Suits!"

The girl pulls both triggers multiple times.

And Ada shoots out a bolt of electricity. She has to stop the woman before she hurts Eric or the others.

The consequences are instantaneous. The blinding bolt hits the girl square in the chest and she screams as she's knocked backward. A chorus of "Akashs," echo around Ada.

And a bullet slams into her stomach a second before she says it herself.

Ada's suit envelops her gasp along with the pain that instantly ricochets through her. But she doesn't have time to process it. Skins swarm down the subway tunnels. Dozens of them. No, more than that.

Hundreds.

"It's a trap!" shouts Logan.

Injury sustained, flashes across the inside of Ada's helmet. *Internal bleeding likely.*

Cassandra shoots out her own bolt of energy, blasting the group of Skins at the forefront. There are screams and the scent of burnt flesh, but the ones behind them simply run over their fallen comrades, shooting.

Bullets pepper Ada's suit, but she barely registers it. Her stomach feels like it's a cavern of pain. She discharges another bolt, but it's not nearly as big as the first. It fries a handful of Skins, but that's it.

It makes little difference against the swarm of evil coming at them.

Body temperature falling. Pulse rapid and weak.

"This is not good," comes Jareth's muttered voice through their comms link. "Really, really not good."

"Retreat" shouts Tristan.

"What?" Cassandra hollers despite their ability to communicate between the suits. She shoots out a bolt, incinerating another dozen Skins. "We've never retreated!"

"They won't chase us above," adds Jareth. "Chardis wants attention as much as we do."

"We're outnumbered," says Brielle. "Tristan's right."

And he is. They've been ambushed by an army of Skins. In fact, Ada would like nothing more than to get the hell out of here.

Except her legs have stopped working. She's not even sure she can feel them. Her entire mind is buzzing with nothing but pain.

The Skins are screaming their lust for Zodiac blood, still shooting even though it has no effect against their suits. Maybe they know it only takes one bullet...

Jareth projects a massive fireball and hurls it at them. The Skins in the first few rows raise their arms, the fury twisting their face turning to terror. But when there's no fire, no burning, they realize it was an illusion.

It buys them a second or two, maybe three.

And it won't work again.

"Out!" orders Tristan. "Everyone out!"

Cassandra grabs Logan's hand and runs. Tristan shoves Brielle toward the stairs, Jareth right behind her. Eric turns to Ada.

That's the moment her legs give out. She crumples to the ground, the impact exploding another grenade of agony through her torso.

Full body shutdown imminent. Assistance recommended.

"Ada!" Eric screams.

And then she's been scooped up, and for the first time since they found the Zodiacs, he's holding her. Ada lets out a long breath, calm flowing through her, washing away the pain even as they shoot up the stairs. She blinks, realizing that it's Eric's power doing that.

"What happened, Ada?" he asks tersely. "Why are you in so much pain?"

"I may…have been…shot…before I could…" She rests her head on his shoulder, her energy fading fast, but she figures Eric knows what she means. They've spent most of their life finishing each other's sentences.

"No," he moans, sounding as if he's in as much pain as she was just a moment ago. "Hold on, we're almost out."

"I'll forge a wall," says Jareth. "It won't last long, but it'll be enough to slow anyone stupid enough to think they should take this above ground."

"I'll stay back," offers Cassandra. "Just to make sure."

"We both will," says Logan.

A few seconds pass, but Ada's too content in Eric's arms. Where she belongs.

"Retract your suits," orders Tristan. "We're almost back on the street."

Ada's eyes flutter open, looking forward to seeing Eric's face. His beautiful blue-green suit disappears. She whispers the word and so does her own emerald green one. How fitting that they're similar shades. Pressing her face back into the crook of his neck, she breathes in deeply. There's no more pain, no more aching. Eric's holding her.

Eric's horrified gasp has her eyes flying open. She looks down, seeing so much blood it makes her queasy.

But Eric's safe. So are the Zodiacs.

In fact, they're all crowding around her. Her arms tighten around Eric's neck. No matter what they want, she's not letting him go.

"Tristan," Eric chokes. "She's been shot."

"We have to get her to the hospital," says Brielle. She smiles at Ada. "You're going to be okay."

Ada tries to nod, but her head is too heavy. Of course she's going to be okay. She has Eric.

"We don't have time," says Tristan, his tense voice sounding lightyears away. "We'll take her back to HQ and use nanites."

Ada closes her eyes, content to ride the wave of bliss while they decide. She's tired. So...weak.

"I love you, Eric," she murmurs before losing herself to oblivion.

25

ERIC

E ric struggles to breathe, his heart feeling like it's imploding into a blackhole of its own making, and it's threatening to suck him in from the inside out. If Ada doesn't make it, he hopes it does.

He's sitting on the floor just outside of her room in Tristan's house as Tristan administers the so-called nanites. Tristan had assured him that everything would be fine, that these microscopic robots have gotten him out of a few close calls, but Eric isn't willing to bet Ada's life on anyone's word.

He might lose her tonight. If Tristan's magic little bugs don't save her, he'll never hear her musical laughter again, never feel the tingle of her electric energy again when she feels frightened or uncertain.

Never get to hold her again.

That last thought shatters the small grip on hope that he's been holding onto, forcing a well of tears to build over the rim of his eyelids.

He's nothing without her, he knows it.

A soft padding of feet approaches him, but he doesn't

look up. He doesn't care who's come to fill him with false promises. If Ada's going to die, he wants to die with her.

Whoever it is lowers to sit beside him, and the scent of lilac tells him it's a girl. It's not the overbearing smell of cotton-candy perfume, so he knows it's not Cassandra, but he doesn't care either way.

She doesn't say anything for a long moment, perhaps waiting for him to look up at her. He's going to disappoint her. Maybe she'll go away.

Her legs pretzel in front of her, her knee briefly brushing against his thigh. Apparently, she's settling in. Nope, she's not going anywhere. Can't she take a hint?

"Ada's going to be okay," Brielle says softly. No, she doesn't just say it. Her voice makes it seem like a certainty.

But he's far from convinced. So he says nothing, still refusing to acknowledge her presence.

She takes in a long drag of breath. "I won't claim to know what's passed between the two of you, but I can tell that you're lying to yourself."

She pauses, waiting for a response that will never come.

"Ada and I have met before," she confides.

This does have him finally turning to her, a question mark on his face. Where is she going with this?

She nods and looks down. "It was way before I knew who and what I was, before I knew about the Zodiacs and just thought I was a freak who had visions of people's lies."

Eric thinks about that for a moment. Is that really what Brielle dealt with growing up? His struggle is nothing compared to hers. Or Ada's, for that matter. He always saw his gift as a blessing, a way to help others by alleviating their pain, and a way to protect Ada by inflicting pain when necessary.

But Ada was always afraid of her electricity. He couldn't imagine what it would be like to be forced to see the truth others attempt to hide. What types of horrors has she seen? He knows the world is filled with terrible people just as much as it's filled with generous, kind-hearted ones, like Brielle. If he weren't so grief-stricken, he'd ask more questions, try to understand this mysterious mouse of a girl.

"At first, I thought she was trying to hide an affair," Brielle continues. "That she was doing something illicit with a boy I liked, so I backed off." She fingers a woven bracelet on her wrist, almost picking at it. "But just before he went away for good, he told me there was nothing going on between them." She looks up at him then. "I know Ada keeps secrets, but I've come to realize that it's always with the best intentions. The truth of it back then was that she was trying to earn money in a way that she knew you wouldn't approve of. But, ultimately, she was doing it all for you. I saw your face in her mind."

She reaches over and places a hand on his knee. "You've always been the most important thing to her. I see that now."

He doesn't want her intimate touch, but he doesn't shirk her off either. Some part of him is dying to hear what else she has to say.

"I've lived my entire life unable to lie, because my power is determined to force the truth out in whatever way possible. But I can't tell you how many times I've wished that I could lie, to save someone grief, to make someone feel better even when I knew there was no hope." She leans closer. "But I can tell you honestly now that you and Ada belong together. She loves you, and you clearly love her. And you're lying to yourself if you think you can go the rest of your life with this wall you've put up between the two of you."

He turns to her then, eyes crackling with a need for reassurance. "How can I put my trust in someone who can't be honest with me?"

She considers this for a moment, pursing her lips before

turning back to him with gentle eyes. "Oftentimes, deceit comes from a place of insecurity. But her heart is always in the right place, where you're concerned. I think you just have to trust that, no matter what she actually says, you're always her top priority. And now that you both know who and what you are, those walls are no longer necessary. I don't foresee her ever deceiving you again."

The walls he'd been holding up around his heart melt, and he knows that Brielle's right. Yes, Ada has hidden things from him in the past, when they had no damn clue what they were doing or how they fit into the world. But now that those truths have been laid bare, there's nothing left to hide. And he's so tired of keeping her at arm's length.

And it's possible he's realized this too late.

"Go to her," she urges gently. "Tell her how you feel. Make amends and start off with a clean slate. You need it. And she needs you now more than ever."

He meets her tranquil green gaze, letting the truth of her words saturate him, giving him the strength he needs to act.

In a sudden surge of confidence and determination, he rises to his feet. "Thank you, Brielle."

She stands, as well, and smiles. "I hope only the best for the two of you."

She walks away, and he faces the closed door, taking in a shaky breath before he tentatively turns the knob and pushes it open.

Tristan stops, looking momentarily shaken by Eric's appearance at the door he was obviously about to exit through.

"How is she?" The words rush out of Eric's lips in an almost growl, and he bows his head in apology.

Tristan nods slightly and whispers, "She's taken the nanites without issue." He looks over his shoulder at where she lays on the bed, limp and unconscious. "It'll take a while for the nanites to work, but she *will* pull through in a matter of hours." He fixes his gaze somewhere on the floor. "I was close to death from an alien poison the first time I took nanites, and they saved me from the brink. Ada is far from where I was."

He slaps a brotherly hand on Eric's shoulder. "She's going to be fine. You just need to be patient." He hovers in the space in front of Eric before nodding once and brushing past him. "I'll leave you to it."

Tristan leaves the room and closes the door behind him, and Eric floats just past the doorway, staring longingly at the only girl who's ever mattered to him.

Her arms are strewn waywardly about her, her usually peachy flesh pale and covered in beads of sweat. His heart jolts inside his chest, rebelling against this unnatural image of her. She should be sitting up on that bed, making a sassy comment to him or beckoning him closer.

As if she really was inviting him, pulling him by her very presence, he closes the distance and perches beside her, casting a yearning, mournful glance down at her ghostly frame.

He finds his hand reaching up to brush a wayward curl from her forehead, his fingertips recoiling slightly at the coldness of her brow. It's like she's barely here.

The cool touch of her hand on his forearm makes him flinch, and he's surprised to see her eyes open, locked on his face beneath half-mast eyelids.

"Hey…" she croons weakly, her voice raspy and dry.

He lets his lips spread in a supportive smile. "How ya doing, soldier?"

"Hangin' in there," she replies, her voice barely audible. He'd still hear her even if his ears were ripped off his body.

The desperate hope in her electric green eyes dissolves

what meager strength he has left, and his lower lip quivers. "Ada, I—"

Her hand flutters on its way up to his face, pressing a tremulous finger to his lips. "It's okay. I know."

He shakes his head. "No. I have to say it." He lifts his head up to meet her weak gaze. "I was so stupid. I should've never given you up so easily. The instant that stone shone, I should've fought for you, not run away like an insecure coward."

Just as she had done for him when he found out about Aqua, he curls himself gently around her, offering whatever comfort his closeness could give her.

"I'm never going to leave you again," he vows against her bright red curls. "I love you."

As if those three words were exactly what she'd been waiting for, he feels her body relax completely in his arms. And for the first time since learning they're Zodiacs, he feels complete.

26

BRIELLE

Hey, is everything OK?

Brielle stares at the text from Kerrim, still on a sort of high from talking Eric into maybe *finally* fixing things with Ada, and this small sign from Kerrim that she's on his mind has a smile spreading across her lips despite the horrendous fiasco in the subway.

She possibly fixed one broken relationship, and her own is right back on track.

Making her way to the kitchen for some privacy with the pretense of getting a snack, she leans over the island and types her response.

Yep, everything is fine. After typing the words, she cocks her head and questions herself. Everything is so not fine. They just got attacked, for pitch sake! And yet, it just feels like another day. Actually, it feels like a win, because at this very moment, Eric is most likely patching things up with Ada. She realizes that she's not lying, and that realization only leads to another of just how insane her life has become—that getting attacked by a horde of Skins could leave her honestly saying, "everything is fine."

She sighs and shakes her head, then continues typing. *I'm sorry I had to run out on you like that. I promise our next date won't end so quickly."*

I'll hold you to that

She blushes, letting her grin explode across her face.

"You seem awfully cheerful." The sound of Tristan's voice has a frown smearing the grin right off. Why does she feel guilty?

She closes her screen and sets the phone down to look up at him as he fills a glass with water from the tap. "How's Ada?"

He takes a chug of the water like he's dying of thirst before responding. "She'll be alright. She looked pretty beat, almost like she didn't want the nanites to work. Like she'd given up." His frown is deep and meaningful. Suggestive, almost, like he sympathizes with her on some level. "But as soon as Eric came into the room, I swear I *felt* a change in her, like hope had been sparked."

Brielle's smile is back, completely without shame. "Good. I advised him to go in and comfort her."

Tristan arched a brow at her as he set his glass on the counter, giving her a knowing look. "Somehow, I think you said more than that."

She bites her lip and looks down. "I might have."

He comes over to lean beside her, fingering his glass between his hands. "I'm glad you did. It was getting really uncomfortable to be in the same room with those two, and I had no idea what to say to make it better." He looks sideways at her with a playful grin. "Brielle, the matchmaker."

"Ha!" If only that were true. "So you're saying that old phrase is true? 'Those who can't do, teach?'"

A serious haze darkens his teasing expression, making his smile flatten. He looks straight down at the glass in his hands, scowling at it like it's offended him. "How was your date with Kerrim?"

She doesn't miss the inflection he puts on the word 'date'. Now it's her turn to look away. She doesn't know how much she's allowed to say about a current boyfriend to an ex. She's never been in a situation even remotely like this, and she has no clue what the modern protocol is.

She swallows and purses her lips. "It was fine." She honestly can't think of anything else to say.

The kitchen is suddenly the most uncomfortable place she can imagine, and the prickling of her skin urges her to flee to a more populated area.

"Does he...treat you well?" Tristan asks, the muscle above his jaw tightening. He doesn't look up at her while he waits for her response.

Brielle's face burns with the blood that's rushed beneath her cheeks, and the guilty feeling is back. She has to clear her throat, even though it's dry as a desert. "Yes, he's very, um...nice."

He nods, that muscle twitching again. He opens his mouth to speak, but heavy footsteps enter the doorway, making them both look up.

Eric is there, for the first time since they met looking...himself.

Tristan stands away from the island. "How's our patient?"

"Sleeping," he says, none of his previous bitterness in his voice. There's even a smile tugging at the corners of his lips, and his brow is completely free of wrinkles. "I think she'll be okay after a good rest. Her wound is already healing." His voice hitches at the end, and she hears the hope in that subtle note.

"Very good," Tristan replies. He looks between the two of them, suddenly seeming very out of place. "Well, I'm going to go down to HQ and see if I can get Esther to distinguish between Skin signals and Zodiac." He makes a funny frown before exiting the kitchen.

When Eric's eyes meet Brielle's, the smile that had been tugging finally wins out, blooming across his handsome face. He shoves his hands in his pockets and strides casually toward her.

"You were right," he says as he leans across the island from her. "I can't thank you enough for opening my eyes and convincing me to let go of my insecurities."

She smiles and looks down as she blushes. She's never quite learned how to take a compliment. "So, everything went well?"

"Everything is perfect." He lets out a happy sigh, like the weight of the world is off his shoulders.

"Good." She can't help but share his joy.

"And since you gave me advice, it really has me wondering..." He leans even closer and lowers his voice. "Why don't you take your own advice?"

She frowns, not understanding. "I-I'm not sure what you mean."

He cocks his head in the direction of the doorway. "With Tristan. It's so painfully obvious that the two of you have deep feelings for each other. I don't understand why you're holding yourself back from him."

She inadvertently lets a snort slip out at that, then covers her mouth with her hand. She shakes her head as she prepares to retort. "It was never me who was holding back. It's always been him. You know about the whole Gemini thing, right?"

Eric nods, a look of "how could I forget" on his face. That's what caused the fracture between him and Ada to begin with.

"No matter how much I may want it, I can never really be with Tristan," she continues, lowering her own voice. The pain at that statement slices through her like a knife through warm butter. "We tried it once, tried to just be together casually, but I could tell he would never fully be mine. Not as long as he was waiting for his dream girl to show up. So I ended things before it could hurt us both even more."

He nods a few times, pursing his lips thoughtfully. "Hmm, well, I think there may be a lack of communication here." He steals a glance over both shoulders as if someone might overhear. "Because Tristan told me that he was just about to make things serious between you two before you ended it. He was going to be all in, no matter what the cost."

This information has Brielle completely blanking. For the longest time, all she can do is stare back at Eric with what she's sure is a dumb expression.

Did she hear him right? Did he really just say Tristan was going to be fully hers, no holds barred? Her heart finally rejects the thought. There's no way Eric heard Tristan correctly. He must have misunderstood whatever it was that Tristan said—although she desperately wishes she could've heard their conversation to know for sure.

She licks her lips and looks away. Ultimately, this changes nothing. If she hadn't ended things and they had gotten serious, it would've only hurt that much more when Ada showed up, even though she wasn't the real Gemini Twin. No, Brielle is certain she made the right choice.

Then why does it hurt so much more than before?

Eric shrugs. "Just...think about it. You never know. Even though he's supposedly destined to meet someone else, who's to say that they'll even be romantic? They may end up being just great friends. And like Ada and I were, she may already be in it for the long haul with someone else."

She opens her mouth to rebut, but he stops her. "All I'm saying is, don't count Tristan out yet. I don't think fate is done with you two." He winks before heading to the fridge, grabbing an apple, and sauntering out of the room.

Now what the pitch is she supposed to do? Leaning over the counter, Brielle feels lost. Aimless.

She shakes her head. No. She can't let herself go back down that road. She closed the Tristan door, and she doesn't even plan to open it again.

But even as she opens her phone to text Kerrim back, she can't help but hear a voice whispering in the back of her mind.

Did she make a mistake turning Tristan away?

TRISTAN

Tristan trudges down to HQ, trying not to scowl. He should be happy. Ada and Eric have finally worked things out and they now have each other. They made it despite the odds.

It's nice to have good news for a change.

Entering the expansive room, he finds Jareth and Veronica there, sitting close as they share a computer. They haven't noticed Tristan enter, and they lean in for a kiss. Although it's short, barely a brush of lips, it's achingly sweet.

Like they're appreciating what they've found…despite the odds.

Just like Logan and Cassandra have. Tristan suspects they're somewhere upstairs, snatching a few moments of privacy. Probably celebrating what they fought so hard for and won.

Despite the odds.

Tristan pauses, his hands forming into fists as Brielle's smiling face flashes through his mind. She was reading something on her phone as he entered the kitchen. She looked…happy. And yet, that's the real reason he can't find a hint of a smile right now. She said Kerrim is a nice guy. She seems content with him.

The scowl contracts his brows and has the edges of his mouth turn down. How the pitch is he supposed to be okay with that? Not when the knowledge punches him in the gut each and every time he thinks about it.

Not when he doesn't trust Kerrim.

Not when he wanted their story to be a 'despite the odds' one, too.

He's about to take a step when the room darkens, disintegrates and dissolves into blackness. He blinks rapidly, as if to confirm that he's now surrounded by nothing. Surely, he can't be having another vision. Not so soon after the last.

But he locks his legs, his torso, his whole body, as he finds himself in space again, bracing himself for what he's about to see.

The pinprick light of stars surrounds him, a vista that endlessly multiplies into the distance. The knowledge that each of those twinkling dots is a planet or a star itself takes his breath away. He's struck once again at how small it makes him feel.

He turns around, wondering why he's seeing this, quickly discovering why he's here.

The wormhole. It's changing. No, it's constricting and contracting. He realizes it's closing, possibly collapsing in on itself. The matter is twisting the blackness, caving in. Like a wave climbing up to the mouth of the abyss.

And the Zodiacs are watching it happen, including himself. As the wormhole blinks into nothing, Cassandra sags in her suit, looking exhausted, and Logan slips an arm around her shoulder. Ada and Eric wrap themselves around each other. Even the possible-Tristan and Brielle glance at each other, floating closer together.

Something must be communicated, because they launch

into motion simultaneously, streaking away, no doubt back to Earth.

To celebrate? The Zodiacs look exhausted, but not beaten. Is it possible that they succeed in saving Aqua?

Tristan blinks, and the scene changes. He's still in space, but it's different, although he's not sure how he can tell.

The Zodiacs are there again, facing the wormhole. But this time, Aqua is a blue orb behind them, its twin-white rings circling it.

They're on the other side of the wormhole. Once again watching it collapse, but this time the wave is rushing away from them. And the Zodiacs are most certainly not celebrating.

Jareth's shoulders sag with defeat. Cassandra throws herself into Logan's arms, burying her face in his chest. Ada and Eric fold around each other, clinging tightly as if they expect to be torn apart any moment. The Tristan and Brielle from this alternate future turn to the other. Their hands reach out to touch, the motion achingly tender.

Or heavy with sadness and defeat.

Tristan draws in an instinctive breath and the scene dissolves. He blinks, finding himself back in HQ, trying to adjust to the sudden change of time and place.

And to what he was just forced to watch.

"Tristan?" Jareth asks, now standing in front of him. Tristan never heard him move, but he must've come over when he noticed him in a trance. "What did you see?"

He asks the words cautiously, almost anxiously, as only Jareth would. Like he's expecting the worst.

Tristan grimaces. He has no idea.

He holds up his hand, needing some answers before he tells Jareth what he witnessed. "Esther, what happens when a wormhole closes?"

"It becomes a black hole, Tristan," she states in her calm

way. "And that section of the universe collapses along with it."

Tristan almost doubles over. In the second scene they're trapped on the other side of the wormhole, watching it collapse.

No doubt knowing it's about to turn into a black hole.

In the second scenario, they all die.

And so does the Aquarius planet. Along with the entire part of the universe it inhabits.

He straightens, hearing Brielle's voice in his head. *The first vision will be the one that comes true.*

The one where the Zodiacs are on Earth's side of the wormhole, all flying home. Alive. Possibly after saving Aqua.

It's Brielle's indestructible hope that has Tristan straightening. "Esther," he says, determination tightening his muscles. "Call the Zodiacs."

They have to get ready. The moment Ada is well enough, they're going through the wormhole.

Armed with the knowledge there's a chance they succeed.

28

ERIC

E ric's spiking adrenaline has his heart drumming out a battle cadence as he listens to Tristan's words.

"I've had a vision that the wormhole is about to change. We have to make a decision about our plan for Aqua. Now."

The entire room is crackling with the tension and apprehension his statement has triggered. And then comes an onslaught of questions all at once.

"How do we know it's safe?" Jareth asks.

"Will we survive the transition?" Cassandra asks.

"Can our suits withstand the pressure?" Logan asks.

Tristan puts up a hand to silence the litany. "In all my visions of the wormhole, we're all there, in our suits, both on this side and the other side. I'm sure we'll be able to go through unharmed. And…we don't have a choice."

Ada rises from her chair to face the computer screens. "Esther, were you able to send a distress call to Aqua?"

"Yes, Ada," Esther replies in her monotone voice.

Tristan sighs and pinches the bridge of his nose as he realizes no further details will come from Esther. "And?

What happened when you sent it? Can you tell if they've received it?"

"I was able to translate their language, but it wasn't possible to replicate their frequencies exactly," she explains. "I have detected no signs to indicate whether they received it or not."

Eric throws his hands down and clenches his fists in determination. "What are we waiting for? Let's go! Akash." His suit bursts forth from his gem to encase him.

Logan steps forward, shaking his head. "We can't just jump into this without a plan. This whole thing could be another trap set by Chardis. We only narrowly escaped his most recent one." His eyes slide over to Ada. "We're lucky only one of us got injured."

Eric's eyes squeeze shut at the sting of having almost lost her. Somewhere under the desperation to save his home world, he knows Logan's right, but his need to take action refuses to let that small voice get any louder in his mind.

All he can think about is his planet shattering in a fiery explosion from which there's no escape. Billions of lives that depend on him even though he's never met a single one of them. A family that wanted so profoundly to protect him that they sent him as far away from Chardis's reach as they possibly could. And it wasn't enough. They sacrificed a lifetime together so that he could grow up in safety to become the protector the Universe needs. Even if he never gets to lay eyes on the parents who sent him to refuge, he'd rather it always be a possibility rather than a finality. He refuses to dishonor their sacrifice by letting them die when he could stop it.

"Of course, it's a trap," Eric rebuts, his shoulder quivering with tension and anger. "Chardis obviously knows we're going to come to Aqua's aid. He knows that Tristan has visions, and he's banking on us knowing about Aqua."

"All the more reason for us to be cautious," Cassandra says as she joins Logan and slips her arm through his. "I know how you feel. It wasn't long ago that I acted rashly to destroy that asteroid on my own, and it was the most fool-hardy thing I've ever done. Hundreds of Skins were waiting for me. Even with my badass fireballs, I would never have made it out of that alive if the others hadn't come to save my dumb ass."

"And I'm not planning to do this by myself," Eric inter-rupts before she's finished. "But I will if I have to."

Ada rushes toward him and takes his armored wrist in both hands. "No one is asking you to do this alone. There's no chance in hell I won't be going with you. But they're right." She waves one of her hands at the group in front of them. "Chardis's assassins *will* be waiting for us. We need to be strategic in how we proceed."

Eric lowers his shoulders, feeling a long, trembling breath slowly roll out of him. "Akash," he whispers, calling his suit back. It withdraws back into his blue topaz, and he feels cold with the air of the room on his skin. "What's the plan then? If we're going to make one, we need to make it now."

Eric, along with every other head in the room, turns to Tristan. It feels strange to have anyone other than Ada leading him. His entire life, he and Ada have been a team, with no one to answer to but each other. And a good portion of that, Eric took the lead, too. Now, for the first time in his life, Eric has multiple people to answer to, with Tristan being at the top. It's been difficult to get used to.

And yet, if Eric had to look up to someone, he could imagine no better leader than Tristan. Even though Tristan's younger than him by a couple years, he has a wisdom about him that only comes with experience and loss. And sacrifice. Eric's certain that Tristan has probably sacrificed more than anyone else here. Because he was groomed for this. Rather than growing up like a normal child in blissful ignorance, he's always known that he was destined to save the Universe, or die trying, and rather than letting ideas of grandeur inflate his ego, he's only been humbled by it. Eric respects the hell out of him for it.

Tristan stiffens as all eyes gather on him, his lips pursing in thought. "As Cassandra pointed out, we can expect a troop of Skins to be waiting for us, most likely before we even get to the wormhole. I'd be very surprised to find no one guarding the entrance from this side."

He looks up at each of them, one after the other. "The first of us got a taste of what combat in space feels like. There's no ground to break your fall, no objects to use to your advantage, and scariest of all, minimal light with which to see who or what might be coming at you. And it will undoubtedly be darker the closer we get to the wormhole."

Brielle, Cassandra and Jareth all nod at this, making Eric wonder what their first space fight was like. He remembers when the asteroid was destroyed by so-called superheroes. At the time, he'd wondered if the footage was some elaborate hoax to cover up some new government technology. Better to let the media believe some rogue agents saved the planet than expose a new tech one country had that they didn't want any others to know about.

Eric hadn't really put the two pieces together until just now. The very people in this room, whom he called his team-mates, had saved Earth from a planet-killer. The knowledge has the remainder of tension evaporating off him like steam from a pot as it cools. If they could manage that, then surely they can save his home planet, especially since there are twice as many of them now.

"So what does that mean for us?" Ada asks, crossing her arms over her chest.

Tristan sighs. "It means that our regular fighting skills

will be pretty much useless in space. We've all trained for hand-to-hand combat, perfecting our ground game. There won't be any ground to roll on, no gravity to give any of us the upper hand. And we'll want to eliminate the possibility of up-close combat as much as we can."

"That won't be hard for people like Cassandra and Ada," Logan muses, rubbing his chin. "Cassandra has her fireballs, and Ada can shoot out electricity arcs. But what about the rest of us?"

"Jareth can use his creation powers," Veronica interjects, putting a hand on Jareth's shoulder. "There's no end to what he can do to fight, only the limits of his imagination. He can form barriers around them, maybe? Trap a bunch of them?"

"And I can cripple them with pain," Eric asserts, the idea sending a thrill through his chest. He wouldn't mind making these bastards suffer to the fullest extreme.

"But that's only for those we can actually see," Logan argues, pressing his hands flat together. "For the most part, the Skins will remain invisible. Those of us without offensive powers can't just sit back and let the rest of you handle it. It would be far too easy for them to sneak up on us and gain the upper hand. So how will we fight? All I can do is manipulate emotions, of which the Skins have very little." He glances at Brielle. "Brielle can only amplify guilt, again, which the Skins don't feel. Tristan, you have visions that you can't control. What does that leave us with?"

A small smirk tips up the corner of Tristan's lips. He walks toward a section of the wall that has nothing hanging on it, and the purpose with which he does so has Eric's curiosity piqued.

Tristan pushes into the wall, and a small square gives at his pressure, only for a moment before pushing back out. Then, seams along the wall that were all but invisible to the naked eye before separate, and a large compartment opens to reveal an armory of fancy guns the likes of which Eric's never seen before.

They're not the crude, matte black of earthly guns. Not plastic or amalgamated steel. The material they're made of is shiny and colorless, almost mirror-like, and yet they don't look the slightest bit as easily shattered.

A gasp choruses from the group as they all narrow in to get a better look.

"I've been saving these for the right occasion," Tristan says, standing proudly beside the hidden armory. "It's too dangerous to use them on Earth. Their blasts, some sort of plasma or something, are too destructive and ostentatious. Not only would they call too much attention to us, but if they were to fall into the wrong hands, Earth governments would try to replicate them. And we can't have that kind of power in their hands."

Everyone nods, still staring in awe at the weapons.

"But out in space, there's little chance of that," he continues. "Those of us who don't have offensive powers can arm ourselves with these."

Cassandra steps forward with gleeful mischief twinkling in her eyes. "I know I have fireballs and all, but I'd still love to have one. They look fantastic! Can I?"

Tristan chuckles with a slight but indulgent roll of his eyes, then reaches for one of the handguns. He extends it toward her, but just as she reaches for it, he rescinds it slightly.

"Hold on," he says, biting his lip. "First, suit up. I wanna show you one of the nifty tricks of these guns."

Pursing her glossed lips on an excited smile, she calls forth her suit, encasing herself in sunburst yellow. Eric can't help but think that she looks like the yellow ranger, and he snickers inwardly at himself, his eyes glued to the exchange to see what happens next.

Tristan hands her the gun, and the instant it touches her armored fingertips, the platinum yellow of her suit bleeds onto it, the reflective exterior camouflaging to her exact color as if melted onto it.

"Whoa!" Cassandra breathes, staring down at it in her hand. "That's seriously frickin' cool."

"Where did you get these?" Logan asks, mystified as his eyes soak up the sight of it before flickering up to look at Tristan.

"Alden had them," Tristan replies. "He must have come here with them, keeping them safe for when we might have need of them. I stumbled across the armory only a few weeks ago."

"Have you used one yet?" Eric has to peel his eyes away from the pink gun to see that it's Veronica who asked the question.

Tristan nods, chewing on his bottom lip and looking down at his feet. "Yeah... I needed to see what they would do, so I took one to a forest out of town." He rubs the back of his neck for a moment. "One shot incinerated a row of trees. I'm not proud to say that I had to set a fire and make it look like a run-of-the-mill forest fire."

Brielle turns shocked eyes on him. "The one that was all over the news two weeks ago? You did that?" Her expression is filled with maternal accusation, and Tristan shrinks a little under it.

"Like I said, I'm not proud of it," Tristan says heavily. "That's why I've kept them under strict lock and key."

Brielle frowns, and Tristan avoids her gaze like the plague. Eric snorts a laugh. The two of them are so perfect for each other, fate be damned.

He feels the need to give Tristan an out, so he asks the question that's blazing in his mind anyway. "You said they shoot plasma or something? How do we reload them?"

Tristan's expression returns to its boyish enthusiasm. "That's the thing. They use the molecules around them and convert them to plasma, or so I've gathered. I don't quite understand the technology, but they don't seem to ever run out."

With sudden intrigue, Ada snatches the gun out of Cassandra's hand, the exterior returning to its non-descript reflexive shine.

"Hey!" Cassandra grouses, but Ada is so lost in her examination of the gun that she doesn't give a damn.

"This is fascinating!" she marvels, turning it this way and that. "I'd love to have Esther tear one apart to master the technology. We could possibly reproduce them."

Tristan takes the gun back, almost protectively holding it away from her, and she looks shell-shocked, like a child who just had their favorite toy taken from them without warning. "That's an interesting proposal, but we don't have time for that now."

The urgency of the situation floods back into Eric's chest, filling it to the brim. "Okay, so we arm ourselves with these guns, and then what?"

"I think the smartest way to approach this would be in a formation that best suits our strengths," Logan proposes. "We have Cassandra and Jareth taking point at the front, as they're both our best offense and defense. Then we have Brielle, Tristan and me in the middle behind them, as we're the most vulnerable. And finally, Ada and Eric holding up the rear and protecting our flanks."

Cassandra spins on him, rescinding her suit, and wraps her arms around his shoulders. "You're so sexy when you talk all military like that."

"That's brilliant," Tristan says, nodding in appreciation. "Okay, before we go, I want you two to get some practice with guns." He nods to Brielle and Logan. "They take some getting used to, and I'm not sending you out there with them before even trying them."

"Huh-hum, you mean four of us," Cassandra interrupts. "I want one, too."

"Why?" Veronica asks. "You don't need one."

"Oh yes, I do," Cassandra argues with mock outrage. "It makes the perfect accessory to my suit. It's an absolute necessity."

"Alright, fine, whoever wants one can come," Tristan says with a wave of his hands, clearly fighting back a smirk. "Let's find a suitable place to shoot. Once we're all comfortable, then we'll head for the wormhole."

Brielle raises an admonishing finger at him. "But no forest fires this time."

Tristan puts his hands up in surrender. "We'll do our best. We should head for the mountain range and aim at large rocks."

Brielle stews but doesn't say anything more as Tristan starts handing out guns. With the advent of this new weaponry, Eric doesn't feel completely hopeless about the fight to come.

Hang on Aqua, we're coming.

29

ADA

The thought of blasting some rocks sounds pretty good right about now. Ada's never had so much nervous energy flickering through her nerves. Without her stone to help her control her powers, she'd be a walking electrical charge. Crackling and sparking.

On the verge of exploding any minute.

Actually, even with her stone the prospect of what they're facing makes controlling it hard. She can feel little pulses dancing over her fingertips, making them twitch. But Ada draws a deep, steadying breath.

Eric needs her right now. And she refuses to let him down. Not again.

They have to save his home planet.

With another breath, the anxiety ebbs a little and the hairs on her arms are no longer standing up. One more and her teeth no longer feel like there's a current running through them.

She needs to save her energy for the Skins.

Ada takes Eric's hand and squeezes it. "We've got this."

He nods, tension making the movement short and curt. "I can't let them down, Ada."

Ada squeezes again, letting him know without words that she understands. Eric spent his whole life looking out for others. His ability to alleviate pain has meant he could help people, give them a reprieve, some peace. The thought that he can't help his people would be killing him.

Tristan heads to the exit. "The more practice we have, the better."

But before anyone else can move, Esther's voice carries through the speaker. "Signal received from the Aquarius planet."

Everyone freezes, but Eric practically becomes a statue. Ada's not sure he's breathing, let alone blinking.

"Yes, Esther?" asks Tristan. "What's the message?"

The large screen on the wall flickers, words appearing across it.

Attack imminent. Defenses weakened. Help needed.

Ada's own breath evaporates. It's not just a message. It's a distress signal.

A desperate plea for help.

Eric jolts into action, striding toward the door. "We need to go. Now."

Ada rushes to join him, her pulse already spiking. She's going to support Eric, no matter what, but he hasn't considered it might be a—

"Unless it's a message from Chardis," says Logan from where he's standing. "So we come running."

"Does it really matter?" Eric demands. "We have to go either way."

Ada surveys the Zodiacs. Brielle. Cassandra. Jareth. Logan. Even Veronica. They all have the same answer on their faces.

She finally turns to Tristan, seeing he's come to the same conclusion as the others.

He has the tight jaw. The resolute brow. The shoulders that tense under the weight of the decision that's just been made in the silent room.

"Eric's right," he says firmly. "We have to go. We can't turn our backs on what could be a message from our own."

A wave of nods move through the Zodiacs as everyone agrees.

Eric lets out a slow breath and Ada shuffles a little closer to him. He would've gone alone if he had to. No, not alone. He would've had her. But with the combined powers of the Zodiacs, they actually have a chance of winning. The likelihood this is a suicide mission has been greatly reduced.

Although not extinguished.

An army of Skins is going to be on the other side of the wormhole, trap or no trap.

Tristan walks over to hold out his hand. "We're bigger and stronger than we've ever been. We'll win," he promises.

Eric swallows, his gaze locked on Tristan's as he grips his hand, as if sealing the words. They all know there's no way Tristan can guarantee this.

But it's what everyone wants to believe.

Brielle joins Tristan, her own hand wrapping around their clasped ones. "Let's save Aqua, just like Tristan's vision foresaw," she adds, her voice quieter, yet vibrating with just as much strength.

Warmth curls through Ada's chest. She presses her hand on top of Brielle's. "To victory."

And then Cassandra's there, and so is Logan. Along with Jareth and Veronica. Hand clamps over hand, creating a wheel of Zodiacs.

"To victory!" they shout, united.

Ada's heart soars as the words ignite the air with hope. Determination. And conviction.

We've got this, she promises herself.

Tristan steps back. "Everyone who wants a weapon, get one." He grips the gun he was holding with his other hand as he grins. "You have until we reach the roof to familiarize yourself with it."

The Zodiacs become a flurry of movement, everyone grabbing a weapon except for Ada. She's never been much of an accessorizer. Her fingers twitch. Plus, she's far more familiar with the weapons she was born with.

A chorus of "Akashs" circle the room and in a blink, the Zodiacs are all in their suits. Tristan in his deep purple, Brielle in her metallic pink, Cassandra in vibrant orange, Logan in dark bronze, Jareth in black, Eric in his breathtaking blue, and Ada in her own emerald green. All looking so strong and formidable. Like a force to be reckoned with.

"You guys look so freaking cool," says Veronica, her eyes alight with admiration.

Cassandra angles a hip. "Which is the bit that matters," she says sassily.

The tension slightly eased, everyone clips their weapons to their sides, the guns instantly morphing to match the color of the suits.

Eric indicates with his head to Ada. "Come on. Let's go up there."

Wordlessly, she follows him. They take the stairs out of HQ, then the stairs to the second floor. At the end of the hall, they take the final steps up to the roof, leaving the door open for the others.

They reach the center of the roof, the twilight sky encasing them, and Ada stops. She reaches out to brush Eric's hand, marveling at how real the sensation is through their suits. "Eric," she says, not meaning the word to be a whisper, but her throat is tight. And an ache is developing in her chest.

He turns to her, his visor retracting. "Ada…"

She steps in closer, doing the same. "I just wanted to let you know, we have to come back." She presses her palm to the breastplate over his chest. "We've never found out what it could be like between us now that I can control my powers."

Eric's sea-blue eyes heat with delicious currents. "We should probably save Aqua in a hurry then."

She smiles, tears stinging her eyes. "My thoughts exactly." She swallows. "I love you, Eric. All my life I've loved you, and I always will."

"We were destined to be together," he says passionately. His hand presses over hers. "I love you, too, soulmate."

The other Zodiacs arrive, and Ada realizes they probably heard every word they said. They're silent as they spread out, once again somber and focused. Cassandra and Logan are holding hands, their fingers tightly interlaced. Veronica looks like she's having a hard time letting Jareth go. Ada wonders if Tristan and Brielle have noticed the way they've gravitated toward each other. Two souls torn apart by destiny, but still wanting to protect the other.

"Ready?" Tristan asks through their coms.

Ada swallows. Less than half an hour ago, Tristan said this would happen once they're all comfortable. Well, Ada feels about as far from comfortable as a person can get.

She's terrified.

Terrified she'll lose Eric, just as they finally healed their fracture.

Terrified they'll fail and Aqua will be destroyed.

And terrified that will only be the beginning of Chardis's reign of destruction.

Resolutely, she closes her visor as Eric does the same. All

those fears are going to have to come with her, because she's part of a team now.

And they've got to fight this.

"To victory!" says Tristan, shooting straight up.

Ada launches into the air, the others beside her. They streak into the stratosphere, moving faster than she ever thought possible. Suddenly, there's no time to be scared. To worry about how this could all end horribly, terribly wrong.

She focuses on the darkening sky the further away they are from Earth. On her Zodiac companions flying beside her. On the data that's now rolling across the inside of her visor.

100 miles.

1,000 miles.

10,000 miles.

With the suck of gravity gone, they travel even faster, a shower of comets streaking through space. For a long time, black night surrounds them, the planets and stars they're amongst feeling light years away.

But then the mouth of the wormhole appears, a cliff into nothingness.

Into the abyss beyond.

"Approaching wormhole," says Esther through the comms. "Subatomic status stable."

Tristan doesn't slow. In fact, his head angles down and he accelerates. Ada's glad. She's always been a rip the band-aid off fast kind of girl. Everyone injects a burst of speed to catch up.

Ada feels the moment they're close enough, because there's a tug, and then they're moving impossibly faster, being sucked toward the unknown.

They're approaching the event horizon.

The point of no return.

30

BRIELLE

Approaching the wormhole is incredibly ominous, making Brielle's bones feel strangely hollow, lacking substance. Not because the gravitational fluctuations are physically doing anything to her body, but because there's no sign of a single Skin.

The Zodiacs get closer and closer, holding their predetermined formation, but nothing jumps out to stop them, no blast comes at them from any direction. It's far too easy. And that puts Brielle more on edge than the fact she's about to do the one thing no Earth inhabitant has ever done before— cross the event horizon of a singularity.

As the perfect bubble of starless blackness encompasses Brielle's field of vision, she realizes her hand is instinctively reaching out toward Tristan. She wasn't even aware he was beside her until his hand found hers and she looked to her left to see him floating there. Even under the thick impenetrable covering of the face shield, she knows he's just as hesitant, just as anxious as she is.

What's going to happen to them when they go through? Will they feel any pain? Will they suffer any long-term damage like radiation poisoning? What will be waiting on the other side for them?

The blackness begins to draw them in, an overwhelming tug in the pit of her stomach and an intolerable fluttering in her chest like the feeling at the top of a rollercoaster just as it starts to dive—only multiplied by a thousand. This is it. They're in the wormhole!

Brielle's stomach lurches as she squeezes Tristan's hand tighter. The only thing keeping her from throwing up in her suit visor is the fact that she can't tear her eyes from the amazing three-dimensional lightshow surrounding them. It's like being inside a firework as it explodes, millions of tiny pinpricks of lights shooting past as the wormhole carries them through who knows how many thousands of lightyears in only seconds.

It's the most beautiful, magical thing Brielle has ever witnessed, and despite the bile reflexively rising up her throat, she can't seem to keep her mouth from falling open in awe of it.

In seconds, the light show is over, the hurtling forward coming to a complete halt that jars every single one of them. Brielle battles dizziness and disorientation for control of her senses, willing her eyes to focus on what's now a very blurry, swirling blue whirlpool directly in front of them.

She blinks forcibly several times, until her vision stops spinning, and the glory that is the planet Aqua shimmers before her with so much more majesty than could be seen from the satellite feed. The thin, almost petite pair of rings that criss-cross around the planet are so crystalline, looking like discs of ice, and she can't help but wonder what they're made of.

"Whoa!" she hears several of the others gasp breathlessly, mirroring her own wonder.

For the longest instant, they just float there, frozen in

amazement as they stare at the first inhabited planet other than Earth any of them has ever seen.

It's not until Tristan's hand loosens from hers and falls away that her trance is broken.

"Now what?" Jareth's voice asks through the coms.

Tristan lets out a long, shaky breath. "I guess...we go down there and try to make contact." She's never heard so much uncertainty in his voice, but she doesn't blame him for it. This is completely foreign terrain, for all of them. She doesn't envy his position as leader.

He descends closer, and they all lean forward to follow him.

"Wait!" It's Ada's voice, and it's filled with urgency. "What is that?"

"What?" Tristan asks, and Brielle can see his head turning as he scans the vastness.

Ada shoots forward, pointing ahead. "There. That dot, floating just above the middle of the planet. Is that a...person?"

Brielle squints, feeling like she's searching for a small bird in an endless blue sky. Finally, she spots it, the unmistakable form of a human body. And it's getting incrementally bigger.

"Could it be someone from Aqua coming to meet us?" Cassandra suggests, hesitation saturating her usually strong voice.

"I doubt any emissary of Aqua would come individually rather than in an armed ship," Logan says.

"Whatever or whoever it is, our visors don't recognize it," Tristan says, and Brielle realizes he's right. There's no little message on her screen telling her anything about the object.

As they stare, trying to make sense of what they're seeing, an inky black substance pours out from the entity, radiating in all directions like an oil spill. The black mass grows, tendrils whipping out like tentacles, and arcs of what look like electricity snap and crackle within the maelstrom.

Through the spiking fear spreading over Brielle's body like venom, she can sense something else. It's so small, so repressed, that she doubts she would've noticed it if her senses weren't so heightened.

Guilt.

Not just any guilt, but one she's encountered before, and once she locks onto it, it's so profound that it darkens her soul just as it did the first time she faced him.

"Omigosh," she breathes, panic crystalizing in her veins. "That's Chardis."

Sharp inhales chorus through the coms, but no one moves.

"What do we do?" Eric asks, desperation slicing through his tone like a knife.

Cassandra floats forward, raising her hands in what Brielle has come to realize as her battle stance. "We fight the asshole!" A ball of liquid sunlight forms in her open palms, snowballing as it spins, and she shoots it at him with a loud grunt.

One of the inky tendrils reaches out to block it, the photons vanishing within the black mass.

"Ah, fu—"

With that, the entire team charges into battle. Cassandra blasts fireball after fireball, Ada strikes out electricity like a thunderstorm, and Jareth manifests rockets and bombs to throw at him one after the other. Meanwhile, those without offensive powers shoot at Chardis with their super guns relentlessly.

But nothing makes it through his spiderweb of dark matter tentacles.

"This isn't working," Cassandra snarls. "We should

surround him, hit him from every angle so he can't see what's coming."

"No!" Tristan shouts as Cassandra motions out of her position. "We can't break formation! There's no way Chardis came here without his Skins, and we can't leave ourselves open to attack. That's what he wants."

"If he brought Skins then why aren't they fighting us instead of him?" Logan barks through gritted teeth, holding tightly to his gun to withstand the momentum of firing it.

"I... I don't know," Tristan says with that same uncertainty that makes Brielle feel like the ground beneath falling out from under her, even though there's literally no ground anywhere near her. "Maybe he's testing us? Seeing what we'll do."

They continue to fire shot after shot as Chardis and his black mass advance on them. The mass is now so big, it eclipses all of Aqua's radiant blue.

A growl sounds over the coms, and though Brielle can't be certain, she thinks it sounds like Eric's voice. As she adjusts her aim on Chardis with her gun's scope, she sees him wince, pausing in his forward motion.

What's happening to him? Has one of our shots landed?

She whips her head around for any sign that someone fired the winning shot, and she sees Eric in his cobalt blue suit leaning forward, hands outstretched and fingers arched, as a low rumble sounds in the coms.

Is he...?

Chardis falters for only a moment longer, shakes his head, then continues to gain ground—or space, rather.

So Eric is using his pain power on Chardis, and because it's not a physical attack, Chardis can't block it with his dark matter.

The most brilliant idea Brielle has ever had flares in her

head, so bright that if it was a lightbulb it would have exploded with its force.

"Logan," she calls. "Stop firing your gun and focus your emotion power on Chardis. Once you find a negative emotion, amplify it with everything you've got. And Eric, push your pain power harder. We're going to hit him with a trifecta he can't block."

Logan doesn't say anything, but she sees him lower his weapon in her periphery just before she closes her eyes and locks her guilt detection on Chardis. It may be repressed under a thick and heavy darkness, but it's so accumulated after so many cosmic sins that it's hard to miss.

She grabs hold of it with her sixth sense and wills it to amplify. Just like last time, images flood her mind and seep into her soul, crimes so vile and cruel that she can barely stand to know them. Whole civilizations wiped out, billions of lives stolen. As she amplifies that guilt, she feels it eating away at Chardis, and the most interesting thing happens. It's almost as if, the more of his guilt that she forces him to face, the more powerful she feels, like it's…fueling her!

"Whatever you guys are doing, keep it up!" Tristan shouts encouragingly. "It's working!"

Brielle opens her eyes slowly so as to not lose focus.

Chardis is crumpling inward, his face twisted in agony. His black tendrils twist and convulse at awkward angles, like they're having a seizure. And more than that, they're shrinking.

He's being hit with physical pain from Eric, intense penance from Brielle, and all of it is being amplified by Logan. They're actually winning! Hope empowers Brielle anew, and she pushes her penance with everything she's got, her reserves being drained and restored all at once.

Chardis rolls into the fetal position, his dark matter storm rescinding into himself.

"Now's our chance!" Tristan calls. "Everyone, hit him with everything you've got!"

Just as they raise their weapons to shoot, a miniature wormhole opens up behind Chardis, a black glass-like orb between him and Aqua, and he disappears into it. Before the hole closes, one of Cassandra's fireballs makes it through. Brielle can only hope it landed on the other side.

"Oh no!"

The words are so heartbroken, they feel foreign in the sense of victory that's bubbling inside her chest. She looks around for who said it and why, and then she sees it.

An armada of massive spaceships is closing in on Aqua, firing huge blasts the size of meteors down on her blue majesty.

"No!" Eric's cry is bloodcurdling, and it shatters Brielle's heart.

ERIC

In desperation, Eric darts forward, determined to stop the destruction unfolding before him. But Ada and Tristan each grab one of his arms to stop him.

"Let me go!" he demands, jerking away from them, but their grip on him is like iron shackles.

"We can't," Ada cries, a hiccup breaking the last word.

"Look," Tristan orders, pointing directly in front of them where a line of Skins is materializing out of the empty space between them and the planet. "We can't fight them, and we sure as pitch can't fight the battleships. We will die if we stay."

Eric continues to struggle, even though his heart has already accepted their words as truth. All he can do is stare impotently as huge, angry red circles cover the blue of his home world.

He's failed. Everyone on that planet was depending on him, and he let them down.

His heart bleeds through his eyes in torrents so powerful they blur his vision.

"We have to go." He feels Ada tugging on his arm now that he's finally stopped fighting. "They're closing in, Eric, please!"

Her voice is the only light in this new darkness, and he latches onto it with the only strength he has left. He may have let his people die, but he'll be damned if his foolishness gets her killed, too.

With a nod, he turns his back on the dying world and follows her toward the wormhole.

31

ADA

The Zodiacs all stand in HQ, their suits still on but their visors up. Each and every one of them is silent as they stare at the large screen. No one says a word. Ada's not sure anyone's even breathing.

The image of what's left of Aqua has robbed them of the ability to move. Speak. Breathe.

Ada can sense Eric's tears even if his face is dry. She holds onto his hand, wishing she could make this easier somehow. Late at night, when they'd climb into bed together and whisper about the impossible things they could do, Eric used to imagine they were from outer space. Even going as far as imagining his home planet and what it might be like. About his people. About belonging.

And yet, they left Aqua to be destroyed.

Ada barely remembers the trip back through the wormhole. She'd barely seen the light show. Barely registered the tug of moving faster than the speed of light pulling at her insides. Her mind was consumed with thoughts of those they'd left behind.

How many millions of people were about to die?

"They asked us for help," chokes Eric.

And they failed each and every one of them.

Ada tightens her grip on his hand, feeling helpless. She can't stop Eric's heartbreak as much as what's happened to his beautiful blue planet. The armada of ships have left, apparently their destruction complete. The rings of Aqua are little more than shards of white, aimlessly floating through space. The red explosions have left it the color of a bruise, mottled and disfigured.

"Maybe there's some left alive," says Brielle. "Maybe we can go back when it's safe. Tristan's first vision saw Aqua whole."

Ada sends her a small smile of thanks, even though she knows that won't happen. Chardis won't leave anyone behind. His goal is total destruction.

"Sweet pitch," breathes Tristan.

At first, Ada doesn't see what has him stepping forward. Only for it to become unmistakable.

A small crimson explosion on the surface of the battered planet. Then another. And another. Little volcanoes detonate with increasing frequency, joining to become jagged red lines. The bands of fire quickly spread, fracturing over the surface of the planet.

"What's going on?" Cassandra asks, fear making her voice thin.

Aqua's now covered in a network of pulsing red arteries. As if it's shattering.

Ada draws in a sharp breath. That's why the armada left. Aqua is about to—

The planet detonates like a fiery bomb, fragments of blazing blue shooting outward as a fire bigger than Ada's ever seen erupts from the center. It multiplies and expands like ravenous wildfire, devouring everything in its wake. It shines so bright Ada's eyes try to look away but she won't let them. She won't shy away from the agonizing destruction of an entire race of people.

Suddenly, the screen goes black. The satellite destroyed by the explosion of Aqua.

And every life on it.

Eric stumbles as his knees go weak and Ada quickly catches him. She and Tristan lead him to the closest chair where he sits heavily. He drops his head between his hands, his shoulders shaking on silent sobs.

Ada wraps herself around him, wishing for his powers. This is too much agony for one person to carry. Eric just watched his people be exterminated. Behind her she hears soft sobs, Brielle's or Cassandra's, maybe both. Everyone else is locked in stunned silence.

Chardis won.

They failed.

Esther's voice jolts everyone. "Message received."

"A message?" Tristan asks in shock. "From who?"

"From the wormhole," she says. "I am unable to trace the exact origin."

Eric straightens, his face wet and eyes red. "Please relay, Esther," he says hoarsely.

Words appear on the screen, ones that have a wave of gasps moving through the Zodiacs.

People of Aqua safely transferred to the Ark.

"The refuge!" exclaims Tristan. "They got to the refuge!"

Eric vaults to his feet, his eyes wide. He grasps Ada's hands as the Zodiacs erupt in cheers around them. "They survived?" he gasps.

She smiles, her eyes moist. "It seems so."

He whoops as he lifts her and spins them around. "They survived!" he crows, his handsome features alight with joy.

Ada laughs, clasping his dear face as HQ and the cheers whirl around them. Eric stops, allowing her to slide down until her feet touch the ground. He presses a sweet, happy kiss to her lips and her heart swells.

They separate, turning to find the other Zodiacs watching them with bittersweet smiles. Aqua may have been destroyed, but its people got to safety.

"We find the Ark," says Tristan determinedly. "And we protect it."

Eric nods, sobering. "Chardis will be looking for it, too."

So he can finish what he started.

"Which is why we find it first," says Brielle, lifting her chin. No one wants to feel the devastation they just did.

Firm nods circulate through the Zodiacs.

Their work is far from done.

32

KERRIM

The news from his father wasn't exactly what he'd been hoping for, but it doesn't change the plan in the long run. It only proved as a lesson as to just how powerful their enemies are. Kerrim's still confident they will win.

He strides to the bathroom, still hating that he has to live in such meager accommodations. Back home, he was a prince living in a palace the likes of which these *people*—if you could even call them that—couldn't even fathom. But it's a necessary sacrifice, and one he's proud to suffer for the cause.

When he reaches the mirror, he smiles at his reflection. It's been nice to be himself for a change. The face he was born with is apparently universally attractive, and it's suited his purposes well on this current mission.

But he knows he won't be seeing much of it going forward.

As he locks eyes with his reflection, he focuses on his intentions. The dark matter around him stirs and goes to work, morphing the face looking back at him into a slightly less handsome boy with longer brown hair and brown eyes.

This face is one he hasn't worn in years.

"Hello, Carlton," he says, flaring a brow. "Not that I'll need you ever again, but you certainly do bring back memories."

And this time, he won't fail with Brielle again.

"Let's try out a new look." Carlton's face transforms, dark matter morphing the masculine jaw into a more slender curve and making the short brown hair grow out into a wild mass of red curls. Suddenly, his old employee turned enemy, Ada, is winking back at him. "Excellent," he says, his voice perfectly mimicking hers.

His reflection returns to its true form and he turns away, picking up his communicator and tapping the desired contact on his screen. He raises it to his ear and says, "Game on."

Ready for the next installment in the Zodiac Guardians series? Check out SAGITTARIUS CHARMED!

SAGITTARIUS CHARMED

Twelve teens. One task.
Save the Universe.

Shreya's never questioned her good luck. The right things seem to come to her just when she needs them. Until several others enter her life, calling themselves Zodiac Guardians.

Insisting she's one of them.

And they're desperately trying to save not only Earth, but an Ark wandering in space, filled with refugees fleeing Chardis's trail of destruction. To do that, they need to find the Staff. Its power can tip the balance in the fight of good against evil.

But the Staff is in three pieces, hidden throughout the city. And for some reason, the Zodiacs are fracturing. Friendships are dissolving. Families are in tatters. Relationships are straining under the pressure. None of them realize there's a threat growing from within, undermining everything they've worked for.

To find the Staff and save the Ark, the Zodiacs need to come together once more. They have Shreya's good luck. But will it be enough?

Grab your copy HERE!

mybook.to/AquariusUndone

MORE EPIC ROMANCE TO FALL IN
LOVE WITH!

ALSO BY TAMAR SLOAN

PRIME PROPHECY SERIES
KEEPERS OF THE GRAIL
KEEPERS OF THE CHALICE
KEEPERS OF THE LIGHT
KEEPERS OF EXCALIBUR
DESTINED DEMIGODS
ELEMENTAL GAMES
THE SOVEREIGN CODE
THE THAW CHRONICLES

ALSO BY TRICIA BARR

THE MATING GAMES
THE BOUND ONE SERIES
THE AMARANT SERIES
SHIFTER ACADEMY
HEAVENLY SINNERS

ABOUT THE AUTHORS

By day, Tricia is a full time mom to two beautiful girls and a wife/business partner to a handsome hard-working husband. By night—and nap times—she's a USA Today Best-selling Author of unique and thrilling teen and adult fantasies inspired by her vivid, somewhat creepy dreams and her own adventures around the world.

Tamar hasn't decided whether she's a psychologist who loves writing, or a writer with a lifelong fascination with psychology. She must've been someone pretty awesome in a previous life (past life regression indicates a Care Bear), because she gets to do both. When not reading, writing, or working with teens, Tamar can be found with her husband and two sons enjoying country life in their small slice of the Australian bush.

www.ingramcontent.com/pod-product-compliance
Lightning Source LLC
Chambersburg PA
CBHW030306180626
46810CB00003B/936